IN

Ensenada

Tess

Seasons Press LLC

Copyright 2018 Tess Summers

Published: 2018

ISBN: 9781792700668

Published by Seasons Press LLC.

Copyright © 2018, Tess Summers.

Edited by Elayne Morgan, Serenity Editing Services.

Cover by OliviaProDesign.

All rights reserved. No part of this publication may be reproduced, stored in a retrieval system, or transmitted in any form or by any means, electronic, mechanical, recording, or otherwise, without the prior written permission of the author, except in the case of brief quotations within critical reviews and otherwise as permitted by copyright law.

This is a work of fiction. The characters, incidents and dialogues in this book are of the author's imagination and are not to be construed as real. Any resemblance to actual events or persons, living or dead, is completely coincidental.

This book is for mature readers. It contains sexually explicit scenes and graphic language that may be considered offensive by some.

All sexually active characters in this work are eighteen years of age or older.

Inferno

Kennedy Jones

I'm a special agent with the CIA, and I'm good at what I do. In fact, I'm considered one of the best. I can play the role of anyone and eliminating bad guys without them seeing me coming is my forte—which is why I was chosen to take down the head of the Guzman family.

Dante Guzman is a ruthless, sexy, cold-hearted cartel money-man. And now it's my job to study him, learn his likes and dislikes—in and out of the bedroom—so I can gain his trust and access to his uncle, the head of the Ensenada cartel.

I just didn't count on falling into Dante's clutches.

Every second I spend with him he manages to pull me further and further into his world. And the more time I spend there, the deeper I slip into the darkness with him, the more I realize...

I like it.

Dante Guzman

Don't let my good manners fool you—I'm one cold-hearted SOB, and I control the family's monetary affairs with an iron fist. There's no place for weakness in my world. Show weakness, and you die. As simple as that.

So when a petite, feisty, hot-as-hell bombshell storms into my life, I didn't stop to think about the consequences of keeping her. I wanted her, and I always get what I want. Period.

Turns out, the stakes were too high...for the both of us. And there's going to be hell to pay if we're going to be together, to one form of the devil or another.

Dedication

To my readers, especially the ones who reached out asking for this book. You compelled me to keep writing, even on days when I didn't feel like it, and I thank you.

Acknowledgements

Mr. Summers—thanks for breaking down all the boxes from my online shopping when I was too busy writing to go to the store.

Summers Children—I appreciate everything you do to try and make my life easier.

Janece Ellers—thank you for being the best beta reader ev-ah! Your feedback is invaluable, and you always, always find time to read and give a quick turnaround. I so appreciate it.

JM—thanks for always encouraging me and making me feel like I'm the best writer in the world.

Darla Edison—thank you for being so supportive as my writing career takes off. I can't tell you how much it means.

Heidi Jo, Holli Ann, Heather Ann, and Sonni Marie—you're infamous now. I love you all.

My mom, aunties, grandma, and cousins—thank you for always, always, always showing up and having my back. I'm so lucky you're part of my tribe.

Elayne Morgan—thank you for making this book better and making me look good.

To the writing community—you continue to amaze me with your support and generosity. Thank you for everything.

OliviaProDesigns—thank you for another amazing cover.

Everyone I should be acknowledging but am forgetting—it's not intentional. I'll remember once this book goes to print. Thank you for not taking it personally. xoxo

Table of Contents

Copyright 2018 Tess Summers i
Inferno iii
Dedication v
Acknowledgements v
Table of Contents vii
Prologue 1
Chapter One 5
Chapter Two 11
Chapter Three 15
Chapter Four 25
Chapter Five 31
Chapter Six 36
Chapter Seven 47
Chapter Eight 51
Chapter Nine 58
Chapter Ten 63
Chapter Eleven 72
Chapter Twelve 75
Chapter Thirteen 83
Chapter Fourteen 88
Chapter Fifteen 94
Chapter Sixteen 103
Chapter Seventeen 108
Chapter Eighteen 114
Chapter Nineteen 120

Chapter Twenty 125
Chapter Twenty-One 129
Chapter Twenty-Two 134
Chapter Twenty-Three 139
Chapter Twenty-Four 144
Chapter Twenty-Five 149
Chapter Twenty-Six 157
Chapter Twenty-Seven 165
Chapter Twenty-Eight 173
Chapter Twenty-Nine 183
Chapter Thirty 192
Epilogue One—*Slow Burn* 204
Epilogue Two—*Combustion* 207
Combustion 216
Free Book! *The Playboy and the SWAT Princess* .. 217
Operation Sex Kitten 219
The General's Desire 220
Playing Dirty 221
Cinderella and the Marine 222
About the Author 223
Contact Me! 223

Prologue

Kennedy Jones/Ruby Rhodes
The moonlight from the ten-foot windows was the only light in the room. The petite redhead stood hidden in a shadowed corner of the ornate guest suite, still wearing her dress and heels from dinner. She loved dinners on Dante's estate; they were always an event, and usually lasted for hours. Tonight had been no exception. El Jefe Enrique Guzman, Dante's uncle, was visiting, and his nephew had made sure to go all-out to show the leader of the cartel a nice evening.

She took a deep breath. This was it—the reason she had gone so deeply undercover, becoming the girlfriend and submissive of Dante, El Jefe's nephew and main money 'advisor.' All so she could get access to the Mexican capo himself—and an opportunity to kill him. No one else in the CIA had even come close, but she was moments away from pulling it off.

So why the fuck was she hesitating?

An image of Dante's handsome face flashed in her mind. His crooked smile when he looked at her, warm and tender. How he'd stroke her cheek with the knuckle of his index finger while looking into her eyes, murmuring words of adoration in Spanish.

Contemplating what killing Enrique was going to mean— never again seeing the man she had accidentally fallen in love with—she almost slipped out the way she had come. Not being with Dante was going to gut her—figuratively, of course. Although if she got caught tonight, it would most likely also be literally, and probably only after she'd been tortured.

Then Enrique entered the suite and caught sight of her, and there was no turning back. He thought she was there to seduce him, which explained why he didn't shout for his guards on the other side of the door when he noticed her.

His grin was sleazy as he looked her up and down and began to unbuckle his belt. "Ah, an ambitious whore, trying to trade up. I like it, although I must admit, I'm surprised."

She raised the pistol from her side, the silencer already attached. The memories of her last night with Dante were going to have to be enough.

****

Dante Guzman

He looked around his bedroom suite with sadness—he missed her presence in this room already. His little assassin was gone.

He'd known she would be after tonight. He knew his time with his sexy CIA operative was going to end the minute he'd announced his uncle was coming for a short visit. A small part of him had held out hope: hope that she wouldn't go through with her plan. That their time together had actually meant something to her, and she'd choose him.

The only thing he could do was wait and see what she decided.

Dante had found her note—which said simply, *It was real*—before he heard the shouts of his uncle's guards when they'd found him dead. He had purposefully taken a business call after dinner and left her alone to make her choice.

It filled him with regret and sadness that she hadn't chosen him.

'Ruby Rhodes' had fooled him for all of ninety minutes after meeting her. There was no way a woman was that perfect and just happened to sit next to him at his favorite bar, order Macallan Rare Cask—his favorite drink—then *accidentally* trip and fall right into his arms.

No fucking way.

She was good though, he'd give her that. She never slipped once, and her government had done a decent job at hiding her real identity. It'd taken his best IT man and more money than some countries' entire GDP to learn that Ruby's real name was Kennedy Alicia Jones.

In his office sat an envelope full of pictures of her life: where she'd grown up; high school yearbook photos; college graduation pictures; the professional, posed photo of the day she finished boot camp with the Marines; candid family photos... Having seen her humble beginnings, it made him love her even more every time she so effortlessly pulled off her heiress persona. But it also made him punish her harder when they played at night. She wasn't fucking *real*, and he desperately wanted her to be. Keni—not Ruby. He wanted to be more than just a means to an end for her. He wanted her to love him like he loved her.

Fortunately, her assignment was also a benefit to him, so he played into her ruse and savored the time he spent with the charming actress, waiting to see what she decided. Should her CIA gig not turn out, she had a future in Hollywood.

Dante stood in his dressing room, staring at the small, black velvet box in his hand. He'd bought the ring today, just in case Keni didn't go through with her mission. If his uncle was alive in the morning, Dante was marrying her tomorrow night. *Kennedy*—not Ruby. He had resolved to end this charade one way or the other, but the way it had ended made his heart hurt. Kennedy hadn't chosen him. Now he was going to have to hunt her down and punish her—for so many things.

Chapter One

Kennedy
After she reported back to her handler with photographs of the bullet in Enrique Guzman's head, she quickly emptied her fat bank account—the CIA had added a lot of zeros to it as a bonus—and went dark. Only a handful of people knew how to reach her, and even fewer knew where she was. That was exactly how she wanted it.

Starting over with a new identity was proving to be lonely as fuck this time, and she missed Dante every single day. He was haunting her dreams to the point where she could almost feel him in bed next to her, and thoughts of him tormented her even when she was awake. More than once, she could have sworn she'd caught a glimpse of him in the little town where she'd gone into hiding, just outside Seattle. But each time she investigated further, she found it was just a dark-haired man in a business suit.

Just wishful thinking?

Maybe.

But if it had really been him, she would probably be dead, so perhaps it would be best if she wished for something else.

Keni had taken a few clandestine assignments since she'd left Dante's estate, but nothing that kept her away from her new bungalow for more than a few weeks at a time. Her landlord and new neighbors thought she was a flight attendant who traveled overseas. That helped explain her sporadic schedule—being gone for weeks on end, then home for extended periods. It didn't justify why she paid for everything in cash, but she'd been able to get away with no questions asked so far.

The hardest part about being untraceable was giving up contact with her family, even her mom and sister. She hadn't been in touch with Reagan for almost a year, and she hated every minute of it. She missed her younger sibling terribly; it'd been too long since she'd heard her little sister's laugh. But it was a necessary part of staying off everyone's radar. Until today she thought she'd been successful, but that had all changed when she'd gone out this morning for her daily run. Now she was trying to decide if her cover had been blown or if the good-looking pediatrician who lived up the street was legitimately interested in getting to know the new girl in town.

He had come out of his Craftsman six houses north of her bungalow, moments after she'd started her morning jog and fell in pace behind her for a block, then sped up until he was right beside her.

"Do you mind if I run with you?" He was classically handsome: sharp cheekbones, Greek nose, full lips, with blue eyes and black hair.

Hello, dreamboat.

She was instantly on guard. The whole thing was reminiscent of the countless setups she'd done on men for the government.

"Sure, as long as you don't want to chat while you do," she huffed.

He chuckled, barely breathing hard. "I'll keep quiet. I just like keeping pace with someone. Makes it feel less solitary."

"Maybe I'm hoping for solitude," she panted.

He lifted his arms chest-high in symbolic surrender. "If that's the case, please say so. I don't want to intrude." He was still speaking as if he were standing still. *Is this man even mortal?*

"No, not today. But some days I do."

"Noted."

Their feet hit the pavement in rhythm but neither said anything more until they reached the park, and he asked, "Which trail?"

If she was being set up, she needed to stay on the most popular trail.

"Panther Trail."

They completed the two-mile route, filled with other joggers and bikers, then slowed at the park's entrance and eventually stopped. Keni bent over at the waist to catch her breath. At least her good-looking neighbor was now breathing heavily.

"You're pretty impressive," he commented, putting his hands on the back of a green park bench and pressing his heel down to stretch his Achilles tendon.

When she'd finally caught her breath, she stood up straight.

"Thanks," she said, walking to the nearby drinking fountain. After a long drink, she wiped her mouth with the back of her hand then smiled. "Well, thanks for the company," she said, and turned to head back to her bungalow.

"Wait!" he called. "Do you want to grab breakfast? Or just coffee if you're not a breakfast person."

The corner of her mouth lifted as she turned around to assess him. "I don't even know your name."

Mr. Yummy held out his hand. "Bruce. Bruce Parker. I'm a pediatrician at Southern Memorial."

She shook his hand tentatively. "Well, Dr. Parker, I appreciate the offer, but I have things I need to do this morning." *Like figure out if my cover's been blown.*

His smile was polite. "Maybe another time...?"

"Sonni Templeton," Keni said without hesitation.

"Maybe another time, Ms. Templeton. Thank you for letting me run with you. Hopefully I'll see you around."

With a wave, she headed back to her house and her secure internet connection to start doing some research. Was he just the local, friendly, handsome bachelor—or did she need to get the hell out of Dodge?

****

Dante

"I stalled her as long as I could, D. I even asked her to breakfast. She wasn't interested."

The fact she hadn't wanted to go to breakfast with the handsome American henchman—his oldest and most trusted friend, John—made him happy.

"Don't worry about it. They're done." He hung up the phone and waited, watching his computer monitor to see when his little assassin came up her front walk. His men had just left, after planting cameras and bugs throughout the quaint house she had rented in Leavenworth, Washington. Why a Scottish girl would choose to settle in a town that had been remade into a Bavarian village was beyond Dante. The few times he'd been after he'd found her, he'd drawn people's attention—a Mexican man in a German village in the state of Washington wasn't exactly inconspicuous. He didn't want to spook her—it'd taken him six months to find her—so he'd decided on a long-distance approach.

The cartel man smiled when he saw her face on the monitor—her auburn hair pulled up in a high ponytail, no makeup, and dressed in her black and pink running gear. She took the steps two at a time and crossed her porch. Judging by the expression on her face, she was troubled about something. He guessed her morning run with John had set off alarm bells. His suspicions were confirmed when she got inside and immediately began searching online for 'Dr. Bruce Parker.'

Fortunately, Dante had already had the real Dr. Parker's photos doctored to reflect John's image.

His heart soared when he saw her next search. This time it was his own picture that popped up on her screen. She stared at it a long time, even tracing the outline of his face with her index finger and sighing.

"I miss you, Dante Mateo Guzman," she murmured.

"I miss you, too, Bella," he whispered back.

With a louder voice, she continued, "But you really need to step up your game," just before his monitors went black.

His first inclination was to curse, which he did—repeatedly—as he pounded a fist on his mahogany desk. He had sent his best men in. How the fuck had she known—and so quickly?

Slumping back in his chair, he sighed as he pondered what went wrong. Then a slow smile crossed his face, and he shook his head.

His beautiful assassin was a worthy adversary. He should've expected this.

Fuck, he was looking forward to the day he could punish her for it.

Chapter Two

Dante

It'd been a month since she'd disappeared again. This time, no one knew where she was.

No one.

No amount of money was going to help him find her. He was just going to have to be patient until she decided to resurface, or until she let her guard down.

Then an opportunity landed in his lap that was almost too good to be true. He wasn't going to have to seek her out—Kennedy Jones was going to come to him.

"Javier has created a shitshow, again," his uncle Ramon—the new patrón of the cartel—said with a sigh when Dante answered his call. "He's kidnapped a pregnant American woman; some sort of retaliation."

Dante shook his head as he processed what his uncle had just dropped in his lap. Javier was the fuckup son of his fuckup brother, Luis. Fortunately, Luis was aware of his shortcomings, and never made a power play. He was always content to be a bit player, which was why he was still alive and his offspring allowed to be a thorn in the family's side.

"Why the fuck would he kidnap a pregnant woman?"

"It's a long fucking story. You remember his wife, Adriana?"

"Yeah—but didn't they split up?"

"Well, not exactly. She ran off to San Diego while they were separated, but Javi dragged her back here, then went right back to ignoring her. She got pregnant, though, and ran off again and managed to have the kid without him ever knowing. She went back to SD with the kid and bumped into her old boyfriend, who thinks the kid is his. Now the ex is trying to get custody, which is how Javi learned he even *had* a kid—Adriana called him for help.

"So Javi's pissed off that some American is trying to claim his son as his own. Well, turns out the American has a pregnant girlfriend. So Javi goes to the US to get the kid and Adriana—and while he's there he decides he'll snatch the pregnant girlfriend too. He says it's to, I quote, teach the American a lesson, but if you ask me he's just being a macho *pendejo*. And to cap it off, the American just so happens to be a SWAT sergeant with SDPD, so needless to say the heat is on all of us. I want to beat his fucking ass for doing this to the organization right now, especially with things still being so unsettled. Like we need another goddamn target on our backs."

"You didn't sanction this abduction? Bring the woman here."

"This isn't your mess to clean up, Dante."

"No, it's not, but it affects the family, so I'm going to help get it straightened out."

And lure Kennedy Jones back where she belongs in the process.

He needed to start getting things ready for his house guests. His cock moved at the thought of the preparations he was going to make for his CIA *guest*. Oh, the things he was going to do to his Bella.

****

Kennedy

She'd been following the story of the San Diego SWAT sergeant's pregnant girlfriend with interest. The sergeant was a fellow Marine and the details reeked of a cartel abduction, so she wasn't surprised when she got a text on her department-issued phone asking for help.

Cranston: Are you available for a consult? Intel suggests abducted pregnant woman and possible child being held at Dante Guzman's. Williams and I currently at San Diego HQ.

Kennedy: I'm on the next flight out. Send me files of everything you have and call a meeting with all players—8 a.m. tomorrow, SDPD Main Station.

Cranston: Safe travels.

Was she really going to do this? Keni looked at the picture of a smiling Cassandra Sullivan in the online news article and decided, yes, yes she was. And what was the story about a possible child?

With a deep breath, she headed to her bedroom to pack. What does one wear to one's possible execution?

Why, yoga pants, of course. Not only were they comfortable, but Dante always loved her ass in them. If she got caught, maybe he'd at least make her death painless if he was reminded of his attraction to her. Not to mention, they were appropriate attire for the cover story she was developing: She and Luke Rivas, the SWAT sergeant whose baby mama had been abducted, were going to be posing as tourists in Ensenada.

Her racing heart was because of the assignment, she told herself—it had nothing to do with going back to the estate that she had grown to love, or the idea of seeing Dante Guzman again. *Nothing.*

Chapter Three

Dante

He'd actually grown quite attached to his pregnant houseguest. Cassandra was beautiful, intelligent, and considering the circumstances, quite charming. He tried to make her stay as pleasant as the situation allowed, and he did know one thing—there was no fucking way he was allowing her and her baby to be separated and sold. He'd buy her himself if he had to, but hopefully it wouldn't come to that.

Then came another phone call from his uncle.

"The boy isn't Javi's."

Dante wasn't surprised. Cassandra had laughed at him when he'd told her the reason his nephew had taken her in the first place. "All you have to do is look at Lucas to know he belongs to Luke. There's no way he's your nephew's child."

He'd immediately relayed that information to his uncle. Javier and Adriana had gone north to Anaheim to take Lucas to Disneyland and wait for things to settle down before they tried to cross the border into Mexico with him. Meanwhile, Ramon demanded a blood test before agreeing to help Javier any further.

"So now what?" Dante asked his uncle.

"Fuck, *sobrino*, I don't know. Javier's already had a fit—told Adriana he's going to sell the kid to teach her a lesson too.

I don't know why he doesn't just give the kid back—he's already taken the woman. But he's being pigheaded and spiteful."

Damn it. Dante needed to think of something fast to buy some time.

"We might as well make a profit on all this. We'll package him with the baby when she's born—siblings bring a higher price. Then we get rid of all the problems at once, and make back some of what we've spent on Javi's shitshow. I hope you're planning on putting him on a tight leash after this clusterfuck."

"Forget a leash, he's going on a fucking shock collar after this stunt. I don't like this shit one bit."

Dante didn't either. "Bring the boy here; he can stay with the woman until she has her baby. I'm sure she'd be happy to take care of him; she speaks very fondly of the kid. And if he's in my custody, we can be sure Javi doesn't pull any more stupid shit."

"Jesus Christ, your estate is going to be overrun. Do you have the personnel to handle that?"

"How difficult can it be to keep a pregnant woman and a three-year-old under control?" Dante said with a laugh.

"Well, if you need extra men, let me know."

He didn't need extra men; he wanted her rescue to be easy. It would be safer for everyone involved, including himself, if security was as lax as he could get away with without rousing too much suspicion.

Call him a narco with a soft spot for women and children. Well, most women. There was one woman in particular he had a hard spot for. And if she showed up to take Cassandra and Lucas—which he was counting on—she wasn't leaving with them. Keni was a smart woman; she should know that.

No, if Kennedy Jones set foot on his estate, it meant she was ready to serve her penance. And Dante was more than happy to mete it out.

****

Kennedy

The six a.m. flight from Tucson to San Diego got her to the police station with just ten minutes to spare. She had dressed in a black dress and heels, making sure her hair was perfectly in place when she left for the airport early that morning and checking it again in the cab from San Diego International. She'd found it was usually best to appear feminine, almost sexy, when first meeting men she was going to work with. It disarmed them. Especially if they were expecting Keni to be Kenny.

She met with everyone involved with the case of Cassie Sullivan's abduction, which now included Luke Rivas's son, Lucas. Months earlier, the boy's mother, Adriana, had shown up at Luke's doorstep and introduced him to his three-year-old son—a son he'd never known about. He happily accepted the boy, and even allowed Adriana to live with him, as long as it meant Lucas was under his roof.

A few days ago, fearful that Luke and Cassie were going to try and get full custody, Adriana had disappeared with the boy and called Javier Guzman—still her legal husband—for help. She'd let him believe Lucas was his, thinking Javi would help her smuggle Lucas back into Mexico. That had blown up in the woman's face when Javier's uncle insisted on a DNA test. When Javier learned the results, he took Lucas from her in a rage, telling her he was putting the boy up for sale on the black market. In desperation, she had gone to Luke and told him everything she knew, which was how the CIA had learned that Cassie and Lucas were both being held at Dante's estate, waiting for Cassie's baby to be born.

Kennedy had read Luke's file last night in bed. After meeting him in person, she felt confident in her initial decision—he was the right man to take with her to gather intelligence and do surveillance. If they needed to wait for reinforcements, they would, but if she saw an opportunity to get Cassie and Lucas out, they were taking it. The fewer people involved, the less chance there was for something to go wrong. And Luke seemed amenable to following her orders—something she found some men still had a problem with, even though her reputation was impeccable and she'd proven herself time and again.

Through her high-powered binoculars, she caught sight of Dante shortly after she and Luke arrived in Ensenada and set up surveillance on the estate's perimeter. He was walking from the house to his chauffeured armored car and was as handsome as ever—his caramel-colored skin a sharp contrast to his crisp white shirt, which was open at the collar. He wore a tailored grey suit and his black hair was greyer now. A rush of emotions took hold of her—love, regret, guilt, fear.

After surveying Dante's security, they made the decision to extract Cassie and Lucas that night. In the back of her mind, though, red flags were waving like crazy—this was too easy, which wasn't like Dante. Kennedy was good, but she wasn't that good. This should be a lot more difficult.

"Get Cassie and Lucas out of here, Luke. If anything happens to me, you do not come back for me. I can handle Dante." She had reiterated that to him several times, and she said the same to Cassie when she slipped into her room that night.

Kennedy wasted no time with pleasantries once she'd roused Cassie from her slumber, instead launching in with instructions.

"On my signal, you're going to follow me with Lucas down the back stairs, to the right, and through the kitchen. We'll wait at the back door and watch for the guard. When he walks by, the count will be fifteen, then we'll slip out the door and run toward the driveway. Luke will meet us at the second hedge and guide us the rest of the way. Do you think you'll be able to carry Lucas and keep him quiet?"

Cassie was already adjusting the top sheet around her center, creating a makeshift sling as Keni spoke. Quickly fastening it around her waist, the pregnant woman simply replied, "Yes."

Keni grabbed Cassie's arm to get her attention and look her in the eye.

"Under no circumstances are you to stop for me should something happen. I can take care of myself; you focus on getting out of here safely with the boy. Understand?"

Cassie nodded her acknowledgment, and they got Lucas situated against Cassie's chest without even waking him. Kennedy began to pick the lock of the door leading into the hall. The lock clicked without her assistance, and she scrambled back.

She had been right—this was a setup, and she had fallen right into it.

The door opened from the outside and Dante stood on the threshold, still dressed in his grey suit, although he'd lost the jacket. His sleeves were rolled up, exposing the TAG Heuer watch she had given him as a present. Well, the CIA had gotten it for her to give to him, to legitimize her role as an heiress. She knew his wearing it tonight wasn't a coincidence.

"My little assassin, I knew you'd come," he murmured with a smirk, stalking toward her while she backed away to the middle of the room.

Without warning, Kennedy threw a punch, which Dante easily blocked. Then he gripped her wrists and spun her around to pull her back hard into his front. She began to struggle, and Dante escalated his hold to a bear hug.

Without even a glance toward Cassie and Lucas, he casually ordered, "You better go, Cassandra. Luke is waiting for you."

Seeing the woman hesitate, Kennedy barked, "Go, Cassie, *now*." She continued struggling with Dante. The scent of his cologne filled her senses, the warmth of his body and even his hold on her so familiar it took everything she had to keep fighting him instead of surrendering to his touch. But she had to keep fighting; her life—and Luke's, Cassie's, and Lucas'—might very well depend on it.

"Bella, *stop*," he hissed in her ear.

She stilled momentarily, mainly to rest and regain her strength before continuing her battle to stay alive.

"Dammit, Kennedy, I said *stop*!"

That made her freeze. She'd never heard him use her real name. She wondered how he had learned it—and how much of her true identity he knew.

"I like *Kennedy* so much better than *Ruby*. It suits you, Bella," he growled against her neck below her ear. "You don't know how many times I almost slipped and called you Kennedy as I fucked you into submission, but I'd catch myself. It made me so hard, my little slut, whispering your real name in my head while I gagged you with my cock."

His hands cupped her breasts, and he yanked her roughly against his hard body. His whispered words sent electricity through her veins, and she knew her nipples were pebbling as he palmed her tits.

Slut had been one of the many pet names he'd had for Keni when he was dominating her in the bedroom. *Whore* and *bitch* were other favorites, and she wasn't ashamed to admit it had turned her the fuck on. Being owned by Dante had always made her feel sexy. The realization that he was using those dirty names as consolation synonyms for her real name suddenly made her feel cheap. The power she'd thought she held had been nothing but a ruse orchestrated by the man she'd thought had loved her. The one she'd thought she was betraying—but it turned out he'd known all along who she was, and had played her like a fiddle.

He'd been the perfect boyfriend. Gorgeous, polite, caring, thoughtful, even easing her into the submission he desired from her. Kennedy thought about the hours she spent in his arms after they'd had dirty, rough sex. They would talk about everything: his childhood, her fake one—the one she wished she'd had; politics, religion, dreams for their future... It had been so hard, those times when he held her, to continue playing the role of Ruby Rhodes, the CIA-created persona that had been designed specifically to make Dante Guzman fall in love.

Ruby was sexy, sophisticated, and eager to please—all the things Dante desired in a woman, according to the government's research. Things innocent but feisty Kennedy Jones, born and raised in Fargo, North Dakota, had to learn fast if she wanted to play the part.

She'd studied the file on him—memorized it. Dante Mateo Guzman. Born March twenty-fourth, forty years old. Educated at America's most elite boarding schools under an alias. Undergrad at Boston College, MBA from Stanford. World traveler, fluent in Spanish, English, and French. Currently the moneyman for the Guzman cartel his uncle headed, charged with laundering dirty money and acquiring assets. Preference for petite redheads—which was where Kennedy came in. She'd thought her alter ego's name *Ruby* was overkill, but hey, she wasn't the profiler creating the identity.

It had surprised her how quickly she adapted to her role as a sexy heiress sent to Mexico to learn Spanish. Of course, she was already fluent—how else would she be able to do covert surveillance in plain sight? It was amazing how freely people spoke in front of you when they thought you couldn't understand them.

Playing a spoiled rich girl had been kind of fun, particularly because she had grown up in a trailer park in Fargo, studying her ass off to get the hell out of there and make a better life for herself. One with a home that had actual insulation and didn't require the use of the oven as a heater in the middle of January.

What had surprised her the most about her alter ego was how much she enjoyed being used by Dante in the bedroom. How wet she got when he ordered her to her knees and face-fucked her without mercy, relishing the feeling of his warm cum as it splashed across her face when he roared his climax. The contented feeling of being owned as he smeared his seed all over her cheeks with his cock before ordering her to lick him clean, and the eagerness with which she would attend to the task.

For the past six months she had craved him; she just hadn't realized the extent until she felt his hardness against her again. The fact he was probably going to kill her was making her body's current traitorous response to his touch most inconvenient.

"If you ever cared anything about me, Dante, you'll kill me quickly."

That seemed to surprise him, and he tightened his grip on her tits as he rubbed his jaw against her cheek.

"Kill you? Oh, no, my sweet Kennedy, I wouldn't let you off that easy."

Suddenly it felt like a bee had stung her neck, and her world grew dark as she fought to stay conscious.

Chapter Four

Dante

Kennedy was afraid he was going to kill her.

That pissed him off a little—although given her offense, her fear was probably warranted. Had it been anyone else, killing her would definitely have been a consideration. But it was *her,* and it was *him.* He was going to punish her, and he was going to enjoy it, but the chances of him seriously harming her, let alone murdering her, were nil.

However, he was certain his family felt differently. It was best if he hid her away for a while, at least until he figured out how he was going to convince them to let her live.

His cock had been leaking ever since he'd caught sight of her on the new cameras he had installed—separate from the existing system, which she'd hacked. She was as beautiful as ever, and he'd been aching all day to touch her. Nighttime, which was when he assumed she'd make her move, couldn't come fast enough. When he saw her on his monitor, maneuvering easily onto the balcony of Cassandra and Lucas' room, he knew his assumption had been correct, and he was immediately hard again. He was out of his office chair and up the stairs to Cassandra's room in an instant.

Now, Keni's petite body was slumped against him, the shot he'd just given her having rendered her unconscious. He scooped her up, breathing in the familiar scent of her floral shampoo, and carried her through his bedroom and into the walk-in closet that led to the secret room on the other side of his dressing area.

The room's original purpose had been one of two panic rooms in the house, but when he discovered he might get Kennedy back, he had decided to turn it into a playroom, away from everything and everyone. No one would know she was even there until he decided she could be trusted, and he could keep her safe. In the meantime, Little Miss Kennedy Jones was going to serve her penance— locked away from the world, on her knees worshipping his cock.

****

Kennedy

The room slowly came into focus as she opened her eyes. Where was she?

The events of Cassie and Lucas' rescue came back to her, but as she looked around the little space, she was still confused. She deduced it was daytime by the brightness of the room, but how long had she been unconscious? Was she still on Dante's estate? She'd never seen this room before. It was small but comfortably furnished in his elegant style, with neutral colors and plush carpeting that still smelled new. The cameras throughout the room were nestled in the high ceiling close to the small windows—both out of reach, the stucco walls rounded... *Bingo!* She knew where she was. She'd asked Dante a few times about that part of the house when they'd walked his estate and neared the curved walls, which always reminded her of turrets on a Spanish castle. He'd laughed and told her it was just part of the exterior architecture, then assured her the interior had been framed and stuccoed to hide the round walls. She'd known he was lying but hadn't figured out how to access the rooms. She'd been able to deduce that Dante's master suite abutted it upstairs, as did his office on the first floor, but had been unable to locate its entry point.

Keni sat up in the comfy bed, noting the high-thread-count sheets and fluffy white down comforter. Her hands glided over the luxurious peach silk and ivory lace of the gown she was now wearing. At least she was going to be a prisoner in comfort, she mused. Then she noticed the tray with juice and pastries on a small round table for two in the corner.

"Bella, you're awake." Dante, dressed in a navy suit and open-collared white dress shirt, seemed to have appeared out of nowhere. At his arrival, she realized the only door in the room was the one to the bathroom. *Where the fuck did he come from?*

She stood, her bare feet sinking into the expensive carpeting, but made no attempt to cross the room, even when he held out a chair at the small table and gestured for her to come sit. "You need to eat and hydrate to get the drugs completely out of your system."

Kennedy narrowed her eyes at him as she strutted toward the bathroom. "I'm not even going to waste my time pointing out how hypocritical that statement is," she said, and slid the pocket door shut with an aggressive, satisfying *thud*.

Through the door, she could hear him chuckling. "I'm so glad you're home."

Home.

It was funny—and probably a touch on the Stockholm syndrome side—but that's exactly what she had whispered in her head yesterday as she and Luke slipped into the trees outside the estate's walls, and she surveyed the grounds. She'd thought about all the nights she and Dante had strolled the property arm in arm, laughing and talking. How she'd lean her head against his shoulder, and he'd tug her off the lighted path, pin her to a tree, and kiss her senseless, which often led to a clandestine tryst under the night sky. She'd gone inside more than once with grass stains on her knees and elbows. When she'd agreed to help retrieve Cassie and Lucas, part of her had been worried this was a suicide mission, but part of her wanted—needed—to know what Dante would do if he caught her.

She finished brushing her teeth, splashed water on her face, and took a deep breath. She guessed she was about to find out.

Rolling the door open, she saw him seated at the table, looking as handsome as ever. It annoyed her how sexy she still found him. She shouldn't want to straddle his lap, wrap her arms around him, and kiss his neck—he was holding her hostage, for fuck's sake.

He stood when he caught sight of her. She could say this about him: His mama raised him to be a gentleman. A filthy-talking, money-laundering gentleman who loved to yank her hair while he shoved his cock down her throat—but manners counted for something, right? Besides, she rather liked the filthy talk and dominant sex.

But not anymore! Got it, hormones?

"Come and eat, Bella," he said as he pulled out her chair. "You're going to start your penance later, and you're going to need your strength."

She slowed her approach to the table, eyeing him suspiciously. "What do you mean, *my penance*?"

"My sweet *Kennedy*, you're going to have to pay for your betrayal." His words were way too pleasant for the meaning behind them. He leaned in and whispered in her ear, "Just so you know, I knew about Ruby Rhodes from day one. It just took me a while to learn your true name."

She sat down, fighting the urge to cross her arms over her chest like a petulant child.

"Then why didn't you stop me, if you knew all about me?"

He sat down opposite her, putting a napkin in his lap. "Because your mission benefitted me. The fact that Enrique's death was already in the works before you came into the picture may help me keep you alive once the family finds out you're here."

"How long before they know?"

"I'm not sure. I had to report that Cassie and Lucas escaped, so I will face my uncle's wrath. I just don't know if he will come here to do it, or if he will summon me to him. Hopefully I won't have to offer you in exchange to appease him."

"You would do that? Offer me as a trade?"

He eyed her for a moment, and poured her a glass of orange juice from a carafe before responding. "No. If all goes according to plan, I won't be asked to."

"And what is the plan?" She took a sip of the juice he set in front of her, but his answer made her spit it out.

"To get you pregnant with my baby. After thoroughly punishing you first, of course."

Chapter Five

Dante

Her reaction was what he expected. Too bad; it was happening.

While he was taking off her clothes last night, wondering how the hell he was going to keep her alive, an image of her—her belly swollen, with his baby inside—popped into his head, and suddenly, the solution to this whole mess became clear.

Put his baby in her belly, marry her, and say that he'd been in on her plan to kill Enrique the whole time. Letting Cassandra and Lucas go was simply collateral damage to make things look good for her handlers.

Now he just had to convince her to buy into his plan and not bolt the moment the opportunity arose. Because if she did, she was a dead woman walking. Ramon would find her—eventually—and have her killed. The only way to keep her safe was to make her a Guzman and a mother to little Guzmans. His father would be thrilled, and he had even more influence on Ramon than Dante did.

"Why would you want to get me pregnant? You know I wouldn't keep it if you did."

"Over my dead body," he stated matter-of-factly.

She defiantly stared him down with a raised eyebrow, and he sighed. "Oh, Bella. For as smart as you are, there's so much you still have to learn. But make no mistake, little one, you *are* going to get pregnant, and you *are* going to keep it. I don't care if I have to keep you locked in this room until you've given birth, it's happening."

"No, it's not," she hissed. "I'm not having sex with you."

That caused him to chuckle. "Sweetheart, I'm not asking your permission. I'll tie you to the bed to take you and breed you. I'm actually looking forward to that."

He could tell by the way her pupils dilated, the thought turned her on. Still, she feigned offense. "You wouldn't dare."

With one eyebrow raised and a cocky grin, he countered, "Kennedy Jones, you should know better. Not only do I dare, I'll succeed. You're having my baby, Bella. The sooner you accept that, the easier your penance will go."

He hoped she'd need at least a little persuasion. The thought of breaking her, making her submit to his will, made his cock move.

Judging by the scowl on her face, he needn't worry.

****

Kennedy

Was he fucking *insane*?

She wasn't having his baby. She had her career and her future to think about—a child was not in the plan anytime soon, if ever. And definitely not the child of a Mexican mafioso. Forget career-ending, that would be life-ending if the CIA discovered it.

But Dante was making it sound like anything else would leave the Guzmans wanting her dead, and she believed him. She knew the cartel was ruthless when crossed. She'd seen the aftermath of lesser offenses. The thought made her shudder.

So which was it going to be? Death by her agency or death by the cartel?

Still, there had to be another way. She was going to have to escape and disappear again. But the idea filled her with mixed emotions.

Oh, for fuck's sake, Kennedy, the sex wasn't that good.

Liar.

She also knew it was a lot more than just sex with this man. She was in love with him. *Goddammit.* She was a federal agent, sworn to uphold the law; he was a fucking criminal. It could never work, not in a million years.

Right?

"You need to drink a lot of water today, little one. And you need to eat. You've got to be starving."

Now that he mentioned it, she *was* hungry. Looking over the pastry selection, she realized he'd only included her favorites. She plucked a cherry turnover from the tray and put it on her plate while he filled her glass with ice water, then made his own selection.

"I'm sorry I can't offer you a hot breakfast," he said as he cut his cinnamon roll with a fork and knife. "Rosa isn't coming in until later to prepare lunch and dinner."

"You could let me make it," she said with a smirk before taking a bite, forgoing utensils.

"Soon, Bella. Soon."

"Or you could make it."

The mere idea seemed to surprise him. Sometimes she forgot that he'd always lived a life of privilege, surrounded by people to wait on him and clean up after him.

"I will definitely try tomorrow," he replied with a chuckle. He seemed to view making breakfast as a challenge.

He poured himself a cup of coffee, and she handed him the sugar bowl without a second thought, knowing he took two spoonfuls. The air of domesticity between them was so fucked up, considering the circumstances. They actually began a conversation about US politics, something they used to do regularly at the table when she was playing the role of Ruby Rhodes. She no longer had to lie about who she was or what she believed—not that she had ever truly hidden her beliefs from him.

He wiped his mouth with his napkin, then laid it on the tray and began gathering their dishes. He stood and picked up the wooden handles. "I'll leave the water and pastries for you to snack on. Lunch will be served at twelve thirty."

"You're leaving? What am I supposed to do all morning?"

"There's magazines, books, paper, crayons—sorry, I don't trust you enough yet to provide you with pencils or pens—and television with limited channels. Unfortunately the satellite feed is hard to get in this part of the house."

"You mean in the dungeon."

His smile was sinister. "The dungeon part comes later, sweet Kennedy."

He stood in front of the bookcase, and it silently opened. *How the fuck did he do that?*

"Don't get any ideas," he called, not even looking behind him. He didn't have to, to know what she was thinking. "Or I will have to tie you up when I leave, and neither of us wants that."

The door closed quickly and quietly. No wonder she hadn't heard him come in earlier. It was an engineering marvel—and contrary to his instructions, she was totally going to investigate it.

Chapter Six

Dante

As he'd known she would, Kennedy was pressing, feeling, and patting the wall where the door came down. The key was facial recognition—his—on the camera aimed at the door, or his fingerprint on a hidden reader. There was another secret entrance with a staircase leading to the panic room off his office, which had an escape tunnel that came out in the garage.

He was a high-ranking member of one of the most notorious and profitable drug cartels in the world; his precautions were not because of the illusions of a paranoid man. He'd never had to use the panic room or escape tunnel for the reason they were originally built—knock on wood. But *fuck* was he looking forward to using the upstairs room for its new purpose—Kennedy Jones' punishment.

He'd placed yoga pants, t-shirts, and sweatshirts in her chest of drawers, along with lingerie of various colors and fabrics in the very top drawer. No bras or panties though. He loved seeing her braless, and no panties meant easier access.

Since he was keeping her hidden, he was going to have to bring his meals in to share with her. He didn't mind; he found her company stimulating, and they'd always had spirited conversations, bordering on debates, at the table.

If he had more time, he'd stay away from her, even make her eat her meals alone until she was begging for his companionship. Unfortunately, time was a luxury he did not have. Her penance was going to begin this afternoon.

After they'd finished lunch, he stared at her for a long time. Ruby would have coyly tucked her hair behind her ear and whispered, "What?" as she shyly looked away.

Not Keni. She met his stare, crossing her arms under her braless tits to push them up so he had no choice but to notice her stiff nipples under the fabric. *So that's how she's going to play it.* He liked it.

He reached over and lightly traced the outline of her nipple over her top. She didn't flinch.

"I want you wearing something from the top drawer when I return later. You can choose what you'd like to wear, but I don't want you in anything but that. Do you understand?"

She didn't say anything, just stared at him defiantly, so he tugged hard on her nipple when he reiterated, "Do. You. Understand?" and twisted as he waited for her answer.

She smacked at his hand. "Ouch! Fuck! Yes, I understand."

He stood and paused before picking up the tray. "I'll be back at four forty-five. Be on your knees on the bed, with your hands on your thighs, head bowed, and your pussy splayed. I want to see the pink middle first thing when I walk through that door."

"Yes, sir," she said, her tone dripping sarcasm. He knew in that instant she wasn't going to follow any of his instructions, and he was going to make her pay for it.

"Four forty-five, little one," he warned and left the room, saying nothing else. His cock was already hard.

****

Kennedy

Unfortunately for Dante, the drawers in her dresser were interchangeable, so she switched the top drawer, housing the neatly folded lingerie, with the one containing yoga pants and t-shirts. That's what she'd be wearing when he arrived later today, and she'd still be technically following his rules. Well, except the part about waiting on her knees with her pussy on display when he arrived.

She knew she was playing with fire, but she just couldn't help herself.

Which, if she stopped to analyze it, was really dumb. It wasn't like she didn't love being submissive to him. On the contrary, she had relished every moment of being taken and owned by him. But the dynamic between them was different now, and frankly, she felt like being a brat. He wanted her submission? He was going to have to earn it. She wasn't going to make this easy for him.

Or, as it turned out, for her.

She was curled up in a chair, twisting a strand of hair around her finger and reading a sexy book by Robyn Carr when he made his appearance at four forty-five on the dot, according to the decorative clock high on the wall. If Robyn's words hadn't already put her in the mood, the sight of him would have. Fuck, he was gorgeous. His tailor-made suit fit his athletic body perfectly, his perfect face always had just the right amount of five o'clock shadow to scream *sexy*, and those beautiful chocolate-brown eyes seemed to see into her soul.

He started unfastening his belt buckle as he stalked her way, the scowl on his face not making him any less handsome. But she hadn't bargained on the belt. *Shit.*

He withdrew the leather strap from his belt loops in one long pull and folded it in half, tapping the loop end against the palm of his opposite hand as he came to stand in front of her chair.

She swallowed hard before looking up into his eyes. Her voice was barely above a whisper. "Not the belt, Dante, please."

He encircled her neck with it and tugged on the end like a leash. The book in her lap fell to the floor as she scurried to her feet to get upright and avoid being choked.

"I warned you, Bella," he snarled in her ear. Then he hauled her toward the bed and sat down on the edge, toeing his shoes and socks off.

"Strip."

How the hell she was supposed to do that with the belt around her neck, she had no idea; if she were in a less vulnerable position, she'd have asked snarkily. But, since she was trying to avoid having a leather strap against her ass, she decided to do what she was told and began to tug on her yoga pants.

"Jesus Christ, not like that," he barked. "Like you're trying to seduce me."

She stood up and defiantly folded her arms across her chest. "That's kind of hard to do with a belt around my neck."

His eyes were drawn to her tits, then slowly moved to her face. His expression was unreadable, but he relented and loosened the leather, removing it from her neck but keeping it folded in half, tapping it against his palm in warning.

She was racking her brain for a seductive song to play in her head. All she could think of was Def Leppard's *Pour Some Sugar On Me*, a song that had come out when she was like two years old.

Singing the intro in her head, she flipped her hair like she was the star in a music video and started her show.

I shoulda just worn the goddamn lingerie.

Keni started with her pants, and her t-shirt fell to just below her bare ass. She seductively rolled her hips and danced around where he sat on the bed, offering a glimpse of her butt but making no attempt to remove her top.

Judging by his smirk, Dante knew she was stalling with her elaborate dance routine. He let her carry on like Ginger Rogers until he'd seen enough.

"Kennedy," his deep voice commanded, "take off your shirt."

She stopped dancing. With a gulp, she did as he had instructed, and stood stark naked just out of his reach. Starting at her feet, his gaze moved lazily up her body until he reached her eyes. There was a twinkle of satisfaction in his when he patted his lap.

"Come."

She approached cautiously and attempted to straddle him, but he stopped her, shaking his head in amusement and patting his lap again.

"Ass up."

"Dante, no. You promised if I stripped—"

"I made no promise of any kind, my little assassin, other than I'm going to punish you and get you pregnant. Now, get your ass over my knee or I'm going to use the belt. I think I would enjoy marking your flesh with leather, so you have exactly four seconds. Three, two..."

She scrambled into position on his lap and braced herself for the first blow. But instead of spanking her, he reverently rubbed her soft flesh in circles, then squeezed.

"My beautiful Bella," he whispered. "I've dreamed of this moment for seven long months."

Keni fought back a whimper. She'd missed his touch equally as long.

She flinched at the first crack of his palm against her ass; the sound of it surprised her more than the smack itself hurt her. He continued with alternating slaps to each cheek, twelve in total. When her skin was sufficiently warm, he followed with caressing her pink flesh while murmuring words of adoration in Spanish.

She'd always been a sucker for his accent but when he spoke to her in his native tongue, she became completely undone.

He spanked her again—but this time, instead of rubbing her skin when he stopped, he dipped his fingers inside her wet heat, chuckling when he found her soaked. "You dirty little slut," he chastised. "You're not supposed to be enjoying this."

She didn't *want* to be enjoying this, but God help her, she was.

****

Dante

His Bella was in his arms again, if perhaps unwillingly. "Welcome home, my little whore."

"I'm not your whore," she hissed over her shoulder.

"No? Are you sure?" He plunged another finger into her. "Your body knows who it belongs to, even if your mind seems to have forgotten. Don't worry, Bella, I'm going to have a good time helping you remember. Look how easily your cunt has welcomed me back. Mmm, you really are my slut, aren't you, *Kennedy*? You've missed your master's touch, haven't you?"

"You're not my master."

"Little one, you belong to me. You just need a refresher lesson."

With that, he yanked her legs wide apart and pinned her to his lap to spank her wet pussy.

"Your clit is so fat, Bella," he said with a satisfied smirk as he began to rub her in small circles with his index finger—just enough to keep her near the edge, but nowhere close to falling over it yet.

"Mmm, so wet. Listen." He plunged two fingers inside her, fingerfucking her rapidly, curling them to massage her G-spot. She let out a quiet moan, sounding almost as if it were involuntary.

"You're my puppet, slut. Your body does what I tell it to do," he laughed as he flicked her clit again. Kennedy flexed her hips against his hand, probably not even realizing she was doing it. "You want to come, little whore?"

She refused to answer. That was fine; he wasn't planning to let her climax anytime soon anyway. He gently squeezed her throat and snarled in her ear, "You don't get to come until you beg me, bitch."

That elicited a tiny whimper from her. His dirty talk and dominance had always turned her on, although he'd gone easy on her before. Not anymore. He was going to punish-fuck her into the middle of next week, then fuck her some more.

Dante pushed her to her knees to the floor in front of him. Releasing her neck to undo his suit pants, he tugged his boxer briefs down, and pulled his cock out as he kicked his trousers and underwear away from his ankles. He shoved his dick in front of her face with one hand as he grabbed a fistful of her hair with the other. "Suck it."

She looked up at him—those emerald eyes; they drove him wild—and reached for his shaft.

"Ah-ah. No hands." He didn't trust her not to punch him in the nuts, although she was slipping back into her role as his submissive beautifully.

Kennedy opened up her mouth, and he thrust his cock in. It was like heaven. Fuck, he'd missed her lips around his shaft. When she slurped his dick and moaned, he almost fucking lost it right then and came down her throat. It'd been seven months since he'd felt her. He needed to slow down because there was no way he wasn't going to savor this. He'd thought about it too many times since she'd been gone.

She dug her nails into his thighs and dipped her head to lick his taint, making him gasp out loud. "Oh, you naughty bitch." He saw her smile as she sucked his balls into her mouth.

Goddammit, I'm supposed to be punishing her.

He tugged on her hair, pulling her off his balls, and slammed his cock back into her mouth, mercilessly face-fucking her while she made sexy gargling noises as his tip hit her tonsils over and over. She looked up at him, her eyes watering, and he had to stop or he was going to come right then and there.

"Lay the fuck down," he ordered and pushed her onto her backside—pressing on her shoulder and dropping to his knees between her legs, feeling the plush carpet between his toes.

He rammed his bare cock into her womb with a grunt and began to rut her like a beast. She struggled beneath him, trying to wiggle out from his hold.

"Dante, no. You don't have a condom on."

"I know, Kennedy. I'm going to breed you like the bitch in heat you are."

"No!"

Her struggling just turned him on more, and he grunted as his impending orgasm began to crest. With a roar, he emptied himself deep inside her.

"Yeah, take it, little one. Take my seed."

Without pulling out, he went to work on her clit. He remembered reading somewhere that making a girl climax with your sperm inside her helped impregnate her. Dante had no idea of it was true, but it was worth a shot. She began to whimper and thrash beneath him, gripping her tits and bucking her hips against his.

But fuck, he'd promised she was going to beg to come. And the way she was panting as he played with her hooded knot, that wasn't going to be a problem.

"Beg me, Kennedy. Beg me to come."

With her eyes closed tight, she shook her head furiously even as she moaned and pressed against his hand. He began to thrust his cock inside her—to his surprise, he was still rigid.

"You want to come, don't you? You want to feel your cunt quivering around my shaft. Beg for it."

He could feel her stomach clench and her pussy grip his dick tight, and he slowed his ministrations on her clit.

"No! Dante, please don't stop. God, don't stop!"

"Sir," he corrected.

"Please don't stop, Sir," she panted.

With a satisfied grin, he resumed his tempo. Soon she was crying out as her body spasmed underneath him, her pussy involuntarily milking his cock for any remaining seed. He knew he was going to come again from the sensation, and began to pump into her.

"Fuck yes," he growled through gritted teeth, not letting up on her clit. Dante was soon rewarded with her renewed writhing beneath him, and he grunted his second release like a caveman as she cried out, "Oh my god! Yes!"

Falling forward, he enveloped her body in his arms and murmured in her ear, "Oh, my little assassin, what am I going to do with you?"

Chapter Seven

Kennedy
She lay in Dante's arms, her backside denting the soft, thick ivory carpeting, and stared up at the circular ceiling. Absentmindedly, she twisted the hair above his neck while trying to make sense of what the fuck had just happened.

He had turned her into a wanton whore within fifteen minutes. She was not proud of that, but it did confirm what she already knew—she still belonged to him, heart and body.

Don't confuse sex with love—she could hear her mother's voice in her head. And damn, especially not the kind of sex they'd just had. Oh, if her mother only knew, she thought with an internal laugh.

But that was the point. He'd just treated her like a dirty whore, and she'd loved it. And she loved it because she loved and trusted him, which was saying a lot since she'd spent the last seven months questioning whether he was going to find her and kill her. She must have known in her heart that he wouldn't, but the rest of her had still needed to know for sure.

He could still kill you, now that he's gotten his rocks off, the devil on her shoulder whispered. *But why would he have tried to get you pregnant?* the angel on the other shoulder asked.

Oh fuck! He tried to get me pregnant! She tried to scramble out from under his hold, but he just tightened his grip and nuzzled her hair. "Thank god, you're back."

"Baby, can we get up? I think I'm getting rug burns."

His cock had shriveled and slipped from inside her, leaving his cum leaking down her legs and ass crack. He sat up on his knees and pulled her pussy lips apart with his fingers to watch it drip from her opening. "I love how that looks."

"Why did you do that, Dante?" she whispered, lying on the carpet with her legs spread while the Mexican cartel's money man examined his handiwork.

"To get you pregnant." His tone implied, *duh*.

She sat up and wiped between her legs with her yoga pants, then got to her feet. He promptly followed and wrapped his arms around her.

"I can't get pregnant, Dante."

Kissing her cheek, he chuckled, "Wanna bet?"

"You can't keep me prisoner forever."

"We'll see about that."

****

Dante

He felt her sigh and heard her whisper, "You can't."

She was right—he couldn't keep her prisoner forever, but he was really hoping he wouldn't have to. That she'd choose to be there with him and their babies.

"So now what? It's not exactly like we can be together."

He nuzzled her neck with his nose, loving the smell of her. "Sure we can."

She shook her head, and he pulled away to look at her, a sad expression marring her beautiful face.

"Tell me, in what universe could *we* possibly work?"

"Ours. We can choose to live our lives however we want."

"Well, I can't *choose* to be with you, knowing what you do, and I certainly won't have my children being raised this way."

"What way, Kennedy? Educated, well-traveled, wanting for nothing? I had a beautiful childhood and adolescence."

"But what was the price? Your freedom as an adult."

He cocked his head. "I was not forced into the organization. That was my choice. I could have gone on to become a doctor, a lawyer, an engineer—whatever I wanted, and I would have had my family's blessing, as will our kids."

The idea that he chose this life seemed to bewilder her. She narrowed her eyes, her voice going up an octave as she shook her head. "You could have done any of that, and you decided to become a criminal?"

He chuckled. "I saw that I could play a vital role in helping legitimize my family's business, so I can leave a legacy for my children that is not all criminal."

"You're still a criminal, and I'm still a federal agent charged with arresting people like you."

"So stop being a federal agent then."

She recoiled like he'd slapped her. "Why don't you stop being a fucking felon?"

"So are you saying if I stop, I don't have to fear being arrested?"

"Well, no. You could still be."

"Exactly, Kennedy. No matter if I left the organization today, I'm still on the hook for past indiscretions."

She snorted. "*Crimes*, Dante. Your past crimes, not 'indiscretions' like you had a goddamn affair." She stopped short, and he could see the direction her thoughts were turning. He pulled her against him and stroked her hair.

"There hasn't been anyone since I met you, Bella."

He felt his chest become damp where she laid her face and heard her sniffle. Then she whispered, "We can't be together. Not in real life. The agency would never let me live if I left to be with someone from the cartel."

He hadn't thought of that. All he'd been thinking about was how his family was going to kill her if they *weren't* together.

"We have to be, because I can't live without you."

Chapter Eight

Dante

Number One on his to-do list had been punishing Kennedy Jones, followed closely by Number Two, getting her pregnant. While those were still high on the list, the new Number One was convincing her she belonged with him and figuring out how to keep her alive.

Dante wasn't kidding when he said he couldn't live without her. He needed her like he needed oxygen. Having her back meant he was finally able to breathe again, something he felt like he hadn't done in the last seven months.

He stroked her hip and leaned over to give her a lingering kiss on the lips.

"Are you hungry? I told Rosa I'd be having a late dinner, but I can tell her I've changed my mind and want to eat sooner."

Kennedy shook her head. "No, not yet. Later will be fine."

He placed a kiss on her forehead. "I'll be back at eight with dinner." He turned to go, but felt her grab his arm.

"You're leaving?"

"I have business to attend to."

She planted her hand on her hip. "Well, I do too, Dante. How long do you plan on keeping me locked in here with nothing to do?"

He chuckled as he walked toward the invisible door. "It hasn't even been twenty-four hours, Bella. You need to learn how to relax. I can get you some videos on yoga and meditation if you'd like."

The book she'd been reading earlier went whizzing by his head as the door came down behind him.

He picked it up and turned around, the door going back up for him to reenter the room. He stalked toward her, tapping the novel against his palm. It stung to see her flinch as he handed her the book, so he leaned down, kissed her cheek, and whispered in her ear, "I would never strike you in anger, little one."

As he walked back toward the door, he called out, "But I am looking forward to punishing you later. Be on your knees, in the red lingerie and heels, with your pussy on display for me when I arrive at eight o'clock." The door opened and he turned around to make sure she was looking at him. "I will not hesitate to use the belt this time. It's in your best interest not to test me tonight."

The door came back down just as she let out a frustrated scream. At least he knew the soundproofing worked, he thought with a grin. Then he headed back to his office to attend to the aftermath of Cassie and Lucas' escape—and to watch his little assassin try to figure out make her own exodus.

****

Kennedy

She'd been able to deduce that the camera above the doorway was instrumental in opening the door, but she didn't think he'd allow anyone else to watch them, so it had to be automatic. She had observed his movements carefully before he left, and now she tried standing in the exact spot he had stood.

Nothing. Not so much as a whisper of movement. She felt around the walls again, and along the bookshelves, and discovered what appeared to be a fingerprint reader. Probably his backup in case the camera didn't work.

His deep voice came from the walls. "Beautiful, I will tie you to the bed if you don't stop."

"Why? Are you afraid I'm going to discover the way out of here?" she called out, unsure where to direct her voice.

"Kennedy Jones, you are adorable."

She'd show him *adorable*.

****

The door opened exactly at eight in the evening, and he pushed a serving cart through, pausing to admire her on the bed, on her knees in her red satin and lace lingerie, legs wide, hands on her thighs, with her head bowed. She had decided she was going to play his game. It was the only way she was going to get out of here; Dante had told her as much. So she was going to behave until she convinced him to trust her, then she was taking the first opportunity to disappear.

At least that's what she told herself. She couldn't stay with him, even if her heart wanted her to.

He left the cart near the door once it closed and walked to where she was kneeling.

"You look beautiful. Perfect."

Dante walked around the bed, as if inspecting her posture, then paused at her side. He bent at the waist, reaching over her shoulder to run his finger up and down her slit. She couldn't decide if she was embarrassed or proud that he found her already wet. Her submissive position to Dante's sexy alpha was definitely a turn-on.

"Such a good slut," he chuckled before pushing a finger deep inside. "Don't move."

She let out a small whimper, clenching her hands on her thighs as he began to slowly fingerfuck her.

"So wet."

He added a second finger as his thumb grazed her clit. Keni closed her eyes, willing herself not to lean back and expose herself more, or press her clit harder against his hand like she was aching to do.

She must have done it involuntarily, because she felt a smack to her clit, and he removed his fingers from her pussy.

"I said don't move," he chastised before delivering more swats to her clit.

If that was supposed to be punishment, it was the best kind ever. Dante pinched her knot and tugged, demanding, "Come, let's eat."

They approached the table, and her confusion about her role was now front and center. Normally, he was a gentleman and pulled her chair out for her—but playing the part of submissive, shouldn't she wait until he was seated? Was he going to expect her to eat at his feet? Would he allow her the use of utensils?

Oh for fuck's sake. So many nuances and rules.

He sat first, which indicated he wasn't pulling her chair out for her. She couldn't help but notice the erection tenting his suit pants.

Okay, so now what?

Dante patted his lap and gently ordered, "Sit." She tried to comply demurely until he tugged on her knee and positioned her legs so one ankle was wrapped around each of his calves, exposing her pussy to him. He wasted no time resuming his leisurely fingering of her, as he instructed her to remove the covering on the plate and feed them.

There was only one dish, but it was heaping with steak—already cut—mashed potatoes, and green beans. Her favorites.

Manipulating food onto a fork while having her pussy played with was no easy feat. All she wanted to do was lean back and enjoy what he was doing to her. Attempting to concentrate on feeding him was torture, which she suspected was the point.

The sound of her arousal filled the room as she fed him his first bite. He wrapped his lips around the fork with a low *mmm*, and she slowly removed the utensil from his mouth.

"Now you, Bella," he murmured before cupping her tit with his free hand and squeezing.

Just as she took a bite, he inserted a second finger. How the hell was she supposed to chew while he was fingerfucking her? When she had first seen and smelled the meal, she was worried part of her punishment would include not being allowed to eat, but now she would have preferred that.

Closing her eyes briefly, she bit back a moan. *Fuck, that felt good.* She wished it didn't.

She continued alternating between feeding him, then her. Dante was in no hurry with his ministrations, so while she continued to become more and more aroused, she wasn't ready to fall off the cliff into orgasmland. Which was both sexy as fuck and frustrating as hell.

When the main course was finished, she reached for the slice of cherry pie, but he stopped her. He lifted her off his lap and onto the table, then pushed on her shoulder so she was leaning back on her elbows with her legs spread in front of Dante's face.

Using a spoon, he scooped some of the pie filling onto her soaked pussy, then dove headfirst to lick it off her. She wasn't sure if his moans of appreciation were for the flavor of the pie or her pussy. Unable to help herself, she cheekily asked.

"The combination is a culinary delight," he teased in return, then slid a finger into her ass without warning and snarled playfully, "Don't speak again unless spoken to."

If he thought he was punishing her by fucking her ass while he tongued and fingered her pussy, he couldn't be more mistaken. The sensation of his fingers and tongue were quickly becoming her undoing, and her stomach began to clench as she felt her pussy clamp down on his digit inside her.

"Come on my tongue, Kennedy. Let me taste you," he demanded as he replaced his finger with his tongue, and she quickly obeyed, crying out as her orgasm shot through her body like a current of electricity.

"Fuck, you are delicious," he groaned as he continued lapping her juices.

This man—with his Dom tendencies, dirty mouth, and skilled technique—had ruined her for any other man. Dante Guzman, the cartel's money man who was essentially holding her hostage. It had to be Stockholm syndrome.

At least that's what she would be telling herself in the morning.

Chapter Nine

Dante

Kennedy lay panting on the tiny kitchenette table. Getting her off was almost as satisfying as his own orgasm.

Almost.

She caught her breath and, without him saying a word, slid off the table and onto her knees between his legs. She looked up at him with emerald-green doe eyes as she massaged his cock over his slacks.

This woman was his goddamn kryptonite. How fitting that her eyes were the color of the fictional substance.

Undoing his belt, she looked up at him to gauge his reaction. He guessed she was looking for permission to continue undressing him, so he affectionately stroked her hair in encouragement. She continued unbuttoning and unzipping his pants, and he helpfully lifted his hips when she began to tug his pants and boxer briefs down his thighs.

His cock sprang out of his underwear, and Kennedy wasted no time in taking him in her mouth. Fuck, she did know how to suck his dick—swirling her tongue under his helmet, bobbing up and down on his shaft to make him nice and slippery, and pressing her tongue on the vein on the underside of his length.

Dante grabbed a fistful of red hair and pushed her head down as he thrust up, holding her in place as he began to fuck her face. Once again, she looked up at him, and this time her eyes watered as she gagged on his cock. Why choking her with his dick turned him on so much, he had no idea, but it did.

"Take it," he growled as he thrust in and out of her mouth. "Take it all, slut."

Just like she always had, she obeyed. Her gargling noises only served to excite him more as he fucked her mouth faster. He pulled out of her mouth and began to spurt cum all over her face. Seeing her beautiful complexion glazed in his seed was a sight to behold, and he smeared it all over her cheeks with the tip of his cock.

"Clean it," he demanded and shoved his shaft back in her mouth. She readily went to work sucking him dry before greedily slurping his length. It wasn't until she'd licked him clean, and he looked down at her dirty face still covered in cum, that he realized he'd wasted his seed by not filling her pussy with it.

He'd have to rectify that in the morning. Scooping her up in his arms, he carried her to bed where he wiped her face with an extra cloth napkin from dinner. Her adoring, angelic smile made his heart happy, while her red hair fanned out on the pillowcase like flames in the moonlight ready to burn him. The two extremes weren't lost on him.

"Rest, Bella. You're going to need it."

****

Kennedy

She should not have felt as happy as she did when Dante crawled into bed next to her and pulled her into his arms; nor should her toes have curled when he kissed her shoulder and answered, "Of course," when she asked if he was planning on sleeping there all night.

As his lips grazed her skin, he murmured, "I knew you'd be back, one way or another."

"You did? How?"

"Bella, you were either coming back under your own power, or I was going to find you eventually and bring you back."

She rolled onto her side, bending her elbow and resting her head in her hand to look at him.

"You came close last month. Kudos to you. You overplayed your hand with the *doctor* though." She lifted her head to use her hand to put air quotes around *doctor*. "Just some friendly advice: Sometimes less is more."

Dante traced his finger on her hip. "I put you on guard with him, didn't I?"

"Mmm-hmm. But how did you find me to begin with?"

"There are some people in your organization who are looking to pad their retirement, my love. Granted, they didn't sell you out cheaply, but they sold you out nonetheless."

"Who?" she whispered, visibly upset at his revelation.

"No one in your inner circle, but people who had clearance to your file. You were smart to go completely off the radar last month."

"Is that why you kidnapped Cassie? To bring me out of hiding?"

"No, I had nothing to do with that. It was just a coincidence—but I did seize the opportunity when it presented itself."

"Knowing I'd be back, and you'd be waiting," she said flatly.

"Isn't that why you took the assignment?" he said, too smugly for her liking. "You knew I'd discover you and not let you go. Wouldn't you have been disappointed otherwise? You love me and wanted to come home."

He was spot-on, and that really pissed her off. She hated being so transparent. She had just barely admitted it to herself, and was still in the process of denying it. She *had* to deny her feelings. She could not be in love with him.

"You're wrong, Dante. I don't love you. I never did. You were an assignment—that's all."

His body stiffened at her words as if she'd physically struck him, his expression sad.

"I hope you don't really feel that way, little one."

Kennedy knew he was giving her an opportunity to take it back—an opportunity she stubbornly refused.

"How could I love you? Have children with you? You're a criminal. You profit on other people's misery."

He leaned over and kissed her cheek.

"Goodnight, Kennedy Jones. Sleep well." Without another word, he got out of the bed and dressed quietly, while she warred with herself to take it back and apologize.

But she didn't, and he left the room without looking back.

Chapter Ten

Kennedy

She barely slept. Why did she say those things to him?

Yes, he was a criminal, but that didn't negate how she felt about him.

It should, the angel—or devil—on her shoulder whispered. *You cannot be with him.*

That was true. They couldn't be together. How could she possibly be in love him? She'd spent her life bringing criminals to justice. And he thought they'd just be together and have babies? Although, they'd make really beautiful babies...

She shook her head, as if that would jar the silly thought right out of her brain. Her feelings for him were based on mitigating circumstances. They weren't real. None of this was real.

She smelled the contents of the tray before she actually saw the covered platter on the dinette table. The same table he'd had her laid out on not ten hours earlier while he ate and owned her pussy.

Padding across the room dressed in the peach nightgown she'd put on after he left, she lifted the silver lid and found bacon, toast, and scrambled eggs. They were definitely not presented to Rosa's standards, so she couldn't help but smile thinking of him making her breakfast—which promptly brought tears to her eyes. She re-covered the platter, but not before stealing a piece of bacon, then escaped into the bathroom where there were no cameras she was aware of.

Once in the bathroom, she allowed the tears to come freely. She'd fought them all night, in case he was watching her. Sobbing into her pillow would have kinda negated what she'd told him. A few runaway tears had escaped when she couldn't blink them away fast enough, but she'd simply rolled over and wiped her eyes with the sheet.

The sadness she'd felt last night was finally unleashed and her tears turned into soft sobs. She'd been so excited to be in his arms again. It had been seven months and two days since he'd held her all night, and the contentment she'd felt when he said he was staying last night had gone straight to her soul.

Your Stockholm syndrome soul.

When she got out of here, she was headed straight into therapy. That would cure her. It had to.

****

The only time she saw Dante over the next several days was when he dropped off her food tray and picked up the one from the previous meal.

He was polite, asking her if he could bring her any specific books, magazines or movies, but always left quickly, dismissing her attempts at small talk and declining her invitations to dine with her.

She didn't like being dismissed by him, even though she deserved it. He was supposed to want her, dammit, even if she was being a brat. If he didn't, why the hell was he keeping her here?

He showed up earlier than usual with her dinner on the fourth night, dressed in a tuxedo, and the sight of him took her breath away.

"Wow, you look handsome," she remarked. "Hot date?"

He shrugged. "I'm going to be gone until tomorrow, I'm not sure what time, but there are some pastries for breakfast and a small cooler with waters and soda. I'll try to be back so you don't have too late of a lunch."

She couldn't resist asking, "Where are you going?"

"The opera in San Diego."

"Oh." She paused, waiting for him to assure her he wasn't going with another woman. When he didn't, she decided to give her future therapist fodder. "Who are you going with?"

"Laila Hernandez." He offered no other explanation.

Keni knew Laila Hernandez was the daughter of Miguel Hernandez, also known as El Rey—the king. His syndicate and Dante's families were not rivals; rather, they were able to work harmoniously together. Hernandez had temporarily assigned control of his Tucson operations to his second-in-command, while he focused on establishing a foothold in San Diego, with intelligence suggesting he received a lot of his supply from Ensenada.

"How lovely," she said caustically, although she tried to keep her tone even. His not wanting to spend time with her was starting to make sense now.

"I'm sure it will be a nice evening."

Ouch.

"Well, if you can convince her to have your little criminal babies, can I go home?"

His tone was clipped, expression bored. "Your ability to leave is now dependent solely on my ability to ensure your safety. Nothing more. Once I have that shored up, I will let you go. You have my word."

"And when will that be?" she asked, crossing her arms under her chest.

His eyes briefly fell to her boobs but he quickly looked up, trying to appear unaffected.

"I'm having breakfast with my uncle in the morning. I should have a better estimate for you when I return."

"So you're spending the night in San Diego."

Obviously he was; he'd told her he wasn't returning until tomorrow, and that he was going to the opera with Laila Hernandez in San Diego tonight and staying until morning. She wasn't sure why she needed him to reiterate that fact, other than that she was a glutton for punishment.

"I am."

Keni gave him the obligatory *I don't give a shit* nod and cheerfully said, "Well, enjoy your evening. I hope everything goes well with your uncle in the morning. I'd like to get back to my life. And wearing a bra and panties again."

****

Dante

The last few days had been some of the worst ever. His only consolation was that he knew where she was, and that she was safe. He'd had such plans for her in that little room, and watching her in there now, alone, was hard. He wanted to go in and hold her, punish her, fuck her, and hold her some more. He wanted to smell her goddamn neck—especially in the morning after she'd first woken up. He wanted to feel her ass against his cock as they fell asleep. He wanted to have spirited conversations while they ate a meal. But most of all, he wanted her to want him.

He knew she was lying when she said she didn't love him, that he'd been nothing more than a part of her assignment. But he needed her to admit it, and to want to be his wife—stay with him, have a family with him—criminal dealings and all.

If she couldn't concede that, then he was going to let her go. But he was glad she hadn't admitted it yet, because he might end up having to let her go anyway.

He'd approached his uncle about Kennedy's safety the day after he reported Cassandra and Lucas' escape. He confessed their relationship had been real, but hadn't confided that he had her at the estate. Now Ramon was dangling Kennedy's guaranteed safety in exchange for Dante's wooing El Rey's oldest daughter.

"You don't have to marry her, for Christ's sake. Just show her a good time," the family's new boss had barked the previous night when Dante balked at the idea.

"What part of *I'm in love with Ruby Rhodes* did you not understand?" His uncle still didn't have a lock on Ruby's real name and Dante wasn't going to make it easy for him.

"*Sobrino*, you're asking me to overlook a serious offense against the family. You're going to have to offer something in return."

"Her *offense* was in the works before she even entered the picture. I knew all along who she was, about her plan. She'd confided everything to me."

Okay, so the last part was a lie. And a big risk to take uttering it. If his uncle knew he was lying to him, he'd pay the penalty. Dante was betting on Ramon not knowing the truth. The man had his ear to the ground, but he also had a lot going on, so his attention was divided among many things. Besides, Dante had played the whole situation close to the vest—only letting his most trusted people in on the truth; even then they were on a need-to-know basis, and no one other than John had the entire story.

"And you didn't think that was important information for me to know?"

"Ramon, the fewer people who knew, the better. It worked, didn't it?"

"So why did she leave?"

"Her life would have been in jeopardy if she'd stayed. Enrique's guards were out for blood that night. Besides, the CIA couldn't know she had fallen for her mark, could they? She had to leave for her safety."

"Laila Hernandez is visiting San Diego for a few weeks, and her father wants her to stay, since he's relocated from Tucson. Take her out tomorrow night. Show her a good time, make her think San Diego is the best damn city in the world, and I'll take the bounty off your girl's head. It's not exactly like this is a hardship, Dante. Have you seen Miguel's daughter?"

Dante had. In fact, he'd met her on more than one occasion. She was pleasant enough for a spoiled cartel kingpin's daughter. She had perfected the role of *daddy's girl,* and Dante suspected that would translate to her love life as well. And while he wasn't opposed to a woman calling him *Daddy*, the only one he wanted doing so was the one he had locked away in his proverbial tower—who insisted she didn't love him.

He also suspected the most he'd ever get out of Kennedy Jones was a *Sir*. If he told her to call him *Daddy*, she'd probably roll her eyes and call him *Father* or *Pops* out of spite.

And that was why he loved her so fucking much. It was also why he cherished her submission when she gave it to him, and why he enjoyed taking it from her when she put up a fight.

Her jealousy when he'd told her his plans to go to San Diego and take Laila to the opera had been a pleasant surprise. It also confirmed that she was lying about him only being an assignment.

He stopped back in her room before leaving for the airport and handed her a small, pink plastic bag.

"What's this?" she asked with a surprised smile.

"A bra and panties," he said dismissively. "Do you need anything else before I go?"

"How about a key?"

He smiled in spite of himself. He was trying to remain aloof with her, but she made it difficult.

"Seriously, Dante. What would become of me if something happened to you? I'd die a slow death in here, and no one would ever even know."

He had already considered that. He'd placed an envelope with John's name on it in his safe, with instructions to release her unharmed. Granted, it'd probably be a few days after his demise before the envelope was discovered, so she'd be a little hungry, but she'd live. He decided to send his American friend a text telling him to look for it if something happened. Dante was planning on seeing his trusted right-hand man tonight when John picked him up at the airport, but decided it was better not to wait. What if something happened to his plane?

"Nothing's going to happen to me, Bella. Try to enjoy your evening."

He hadn't meant to call her by his favorite term of endearment; it had just slipped out.

She snorted in derision. "Oh, don't worry about me. I'll just be catching up on my emails and working... oh, wait."

"Sarcasm doesn't suit you, little one."

Goddammit. Kennedy—not Bella, not little one. Call her by her fucking name.

"Your saying that just proves how little you know the real me. Sarcasm is my native tongue."

"I know you better than you think, Kennedy Alicia Jones," he said, taking a parting shot before exiting the room.

But not before hearing her huff, "I doubt that."

He hated to admit it—even to himself—but he doubted it, too.

Chapter Eleven

Kennedy

Dante was on a fucking date while she was locked in this goddamn prison.

An *overnight* date. She had to admit it—that felt like a punch in the gut. But, seriously, fuck him. What a jerk.

But it also meant she was unsupervised. All night. Maybe she could figure a way out of here after all—get far away from Dante Guzman and start the process of healing her heart and mind.

Kennedy spent the next hour observing the room and planning, but didn't actually move into action until she felt certain he'd left. She stripped the sheets from her bed and twisted them, tying the fitted and top sheet together to form a long rope. Next, she emptied the cooler Dante had left and tied the handle to the sheet. That would give her the weight she needed when she tried tossing it around a camera he had mounted near one of the high narrow windows next to the ceiling. It was hard to judge from the ground whether she'd be able to fit through it, but she was going to at least try.

The cooler was clumsy; instead of wrapping around the camera, it knocked it from its base so it was hanging by the wiring.

Shit. She had definitely better escape before Dante got back and saw that.

Luckily, there were more cameras and more windows.

She experimented with other objects until she was able to lasso a water bottle around a camera mount. Kennedy moved the bed to break her fall, in case the camera didn't hold her weight, then she gingerly started her climb up the wall.

****

Dante

They'd just reached cruising altitude when he got an alert on his phone that one of the cameras in Kennedy's room had been moved. He chuckled to himself as he brought up the app to watch her.

"That little minx." He grinned as he clicked buttons, then quickly jumped out of his seat when the room appeared on video.

Pounding on the cockpit door, he thundered, "Turn the plane around! Now!"

If he got back in time, he was going to blister her ass. He just hoped he made it before she escaped.

Dante slumped back down in his seat, watching in disbelief and shaking his head as his little assassin went about her breakout. He *knew* what she was capable of—had seen her in action when she came for Cassandra and Lucas—and he still fucking underestimated her. Her tiny stature and beautiful features made it easy to do.

"Fuuuuuck!" he roared and punched the seat next to him.

He was going back to Ensenada to keep her with him until he could keep her safe, but keeping her safe meant he was supposed to be in San Diego tonight.

Picking up the plane phone, he pressed the button for John. His eyes were still glued to the screen on his cell; he was amazed at her ingenuity.

"Get your tux out. You're going to the opera tonight."

Chapter Twelve

Kennedy

Breaking the window proved harder than she'd originally thought. It was difficult getting leverage when she was balancing on two inches of window ledge. She'd deduced she'd be able to squeeze through, barely, even with three pairs of yoga pants on. On her second trip up the wall, she brought bath towels to lay over the frame. Hopefully between that and the added layers of clothing, she'd minimize the risk of cuts from the glass.

Keni hadn't allowed herself to think about how angry Dante was going to be until her second climb up the wall.

Good, fuck him. She'd be back in the States before his date was even over. Hopefully she'd be off the estate before they were even naked. *Asshole.*

Clearing as much glass as she could, she laid the towels over the frame, wrapped the sheet around her wrist and laid flat. The makeshift rope was only going to reach halfway down the exterior wall, so she was in for quite a drop. Keni took a deep breath, rolled out the window, and began rappelling down as far as the sheet would take her. She braced herself with her legs against the brick, took another breath, and dropped her feet away from the building to dangle. With eyes closed, she let go, landed in a crouched position, then rolled. Her training told her to jump up and run, but she lay on the ground, mentally assessing her body for any damage.

"Just what in the hell do you think you're doing?"

Dante's voice was low, but angry. Scary-angry. She'd never heard him sound like that, and a quick glance at his handsome face when he appeared from the trees, still in his tuxedo, indicated his tone matched his mood.

She was up like a shot and running like her life depended on it.

It probably did.

****

Dante

Holy shit, she was fast. The tennis shoes she had been wearing the night she arrived had gone into the closet next to the four-inch heels he'd bought her, and he'd known it was a mistake the minute he put them there. Now, as he slipped over the wet grass in his shiny loafers trying to catch her, he was cursing himself for not trusting his gut.

Luckily for him, his stride was much longer than hers. Unfortunately for him, she was trained in evasive maneuvers and was darting through the estate faster than he was. Each time he thought he'd caught her, she broke stride, dodging this way and that. She was like a little fucking red-haired ninja.

"Goddammit, Kennedy. Stop! I'm not going to hurt you." *Much.* But his commands fell on deaf ears.

They reached a clearing of grass—all that was left once she got past the lawn was the fence, then she was off the property. Desperate times called for desperate measures.

He kicked his shoes off, thankfully pulling his socks off in the process, and broke into a sprint after her, tackling her before she reached the brick barrier.

She kicked and punched, but finally he was straddling her on the ground with her arms pinned above her head. They both stared at each other with chests heaving, unable to speak as they panted from exertion.

Finally, he huffed, "What the fuck were you thinking? You could have killed yourself with that stunt."

Her breathing was still heavy, and she simply shook her head.

Lowering his face inches from hers, he growled, "I can't lose you again, Bella."

Out of the blue, she attempted a maneuver straight out of the MMA, attempting to wrap her legs around his neck from behind and flip him over. Unfortunately, he was too tall for her to pull it off.

"Would you knock it off?"

Her wiggling and struggling was making his cock hard, and her vulnerable position wasn't helping matters.

"Damn it, woman," he snarled before planting his lips on hers. Her response was instant. He hadn't expected her to return the kiss so easily, so he was immediately on guard. She whimpered and pressed her hips up as he pressed his down.

Holding her wrists in one hand, he dropped onto his elbow and stretched his legs out so his body enveloped hers completely, their pelvic bones crushed together as he deepened the kiss. They were soon breathing heavily again, for an entirely different reason.

He needed to be inside her—now. The way she was fumbling with his belt, she was either setting him up or she felt the same. *Why the fuck does she have so many pairs of pants on??*

They were soon naked from the waist down and with one swift motion, he was inside her wet, inviting pussy. She bucked her hips up to meet him, and they both moaned as he filled her completely. His thrusts were slow but steady while he hugged her upper body and nuzzled her neck.

"You feel so good," she whispered.

"Don't leave me, Bella," he growled, pulling her tightly against him and thrusting harder. "I need you."

She didn't respond, just moaned her appreciation at his efforts.

"You belong with me, little one."

He leaned down and kissed her. She hadn't answered verbally, but the way she clung to him told him what he needed to know.

Plunging into her pussy, he hit her clit with each upward thrust and each slide back until she wrapped her legs around the backs of his thighs. Thrashing her shoulders, she called out his name in ecstasy. He loved how her pussy got tighter around his cock when she came.

"I'm ruined for any other man," she sighed underneath him, his stiff cock still buried inside her.

"That's good, because you're never going to be with another man."

Once again, she didn't reply.

Nuzzling her neck and breathing her in, he whispered, "Baby, you can't leave me. It's not safe."

"Why do you care, Dante?" Her voice was soft but strong.

He lifted his head so he was looking her in the eye. "I love you. If something ever happened to you, I don't know how I'd survive."

She snorted. "If you love me so much, why were you taking Laila Hernandez to the opera?"

"Because my uncle said if I made her happy, he'd take the bounty off your head."

She paused for a moment, slowly digesting what he'd said.

"And I screwed that up," she sighed knowingly, her fingers twirling the hair at his collar.

He chuckled as he removed his tux jacket and set it in the grass next to them.

"I sent John in my place. I don't think she'll complain."

"Who's John?"

"John Turner, my right-hand man in America. You met him."

Her furrowed brow indicated she wasn't making the connection.

"Dr. Bruce Parker. Your jogging partner."

"Ohhhhh. Yeah, he's a *very* nice consolation prize for Dante Guzman. Good pick."

He tickled her sides, growling, "Oh, you think so, huh?"

She erupted in squeals and tried to move his hands, resulting in them wrestling and switching positions so she was on top of him, his dick still inside her. Dante grabbed his jacket and covered her bare ass with it; she didn't need to give one of his guards an eyeful, should they be discovered.

As if on cue, he was blinded by a bright light. Using the lapels of his jacket, he pulled her face into the crook of his neck to hide her from his security man's view, and wrapped his hand around the back of her head. With his other hand, he shielded his eyes.

"Mr. Guzman? Is that you?"

"Yes, Eduardo. It's me."

He heard the soft click of the safety on the AR15 being engaged, and the light was immediately turned off.

"I'm sorry, sir. I wasn't expecting anyone to be out here."

"We just decided to go for a stroll." Dante didn't point out the obvious—that they were sprawled out on the grass, not *strolling*. Eduardo was smart enough to not to mention it either.

"I'll, uh, just continue my rounds."

"Thanks. Why don't you skip this sector on your next pass."

They lay still for a few moments. Then Kennedy rested on her elbows and looked down at him, giggling, and it melted his fucking heart. Cupping her face, he pulled her mouth to his. Just as before, she immediately returned his kiss, and once again, he became lost in her. She began to roll her hips against his while unbuttoning his shirt, and yanked it open once the last button was undone. Dante tugged her t-shirt and sports bra off her, and she fell forward, making them both moan out loud when her bare skin came in contact with his.

She started to kiss from his neck down to his chest, her stiff nipples grazing his core as she moved her hips to situate herself further down his thighs, the better to kiss and lick his nipples. His fingers tangled in her hair, caressing her scalp, and he began to slowly move inside her.

Dante stroked her cheek with his knuckle. "Bella, you could have been killed. Is being here with me so terrible that you had to literally climb the walls and jump out a window?"

"Do you really want to have this conversation right now?" she asked as she subtly moved her hips in circles.

His cock was buried inside her, yet he was warring with himself. He *did* want to have this conversation right now, but he also wanted to keep fucking her.

"Yes," he replied, but not pulling out.

"You weren't here with me, remember? You were on a *date*. And I was going crazy in that room. I can't go back in there, Dante." She continued delicately riding his cock.

He tucked her hair behind her ear, then briefly closed his eyes to relish how good she felt.

"Can I trust you to stay with me? At least until I get things with my uncle squared away. Then it will be your decision if you remain here or leave. I won't force you to be here if you don't want to be."

"I promise," she whispered, then started to roll her hips more vigorously, temporarily leaving him speechless. Her pebbled nipples were sexy as fuck and her pussy felt so damn good. "Let me know when you're going to come."

He started to manipulate her clit with his fingers. "Just concentrate on you, baby. I'm not going to until you do, and I promise I'll pull out when I do."

She was a fucking sex goddess, taking her pleasure as she rode him unabandoned, and he was having a hard time keeping his promise. Mercifully, her cunt soon began to quiver around his cock, and she made soft noises as she climaxed. Dante gripped her hips tight and began to thrust hard and deep into her before lifting her ass off him and spurting onto his stomach with quiet grunts.

Kennedy slid along his side and sighed contently when she nestled her naked body next to his, using his tux jacket as a blanket.

He stroked her hair and whispered, "Come on, Bella. Let's go inside."

Chapter Thirteen

Kennedy

They stood and gathered their clothes, Dante dressed much faster than she did, partly because she was trying to separate three pairs of yoga pants. Impatiently, he scooped her up and threw her over his shoulder, her bare ass on display for anyone to see as they walked past—though she knew his servants and staff were smart enough to make themselves scarce.

She loved that he always took charge. From the first day she'd met him, when he wanted something done, it got done. He made sure of it, oftentimes handling it personally.

He marched up the stairs and into his room, tossing her on his bed so her body bounced before he raised her arms over her head and nuzzled her neck again. Slowly, he pulled away and leaned back to take her in under the glow of his bedroom lights.

"My beautiful, Kennedy. Back in my bed where you belong." The way he uttered her name was almost reverent, and it made her skin break out in goose pimples while her nipples stiffened. He noticed the tiny dots on her flesh and laughed. "That's my girl."

Keni was relishing being Dante's girl again—so much so that she didn't comprehend the handcuff on her left wrist until it was fastened to the headboard.

"What are you doing?" she huffed.

"Just in case you're thinking about killing me tonight."

"*Are you serious?* You know I'm not going to do that."

"Well, my little assassin, I can't be too sure." He leaned over to shut the bedside lamp off, pausing to tell her, "Goodnight, Bella. Sweet dreams."

"Goddammit, Dante, no. I have to pee, for Chrissake, and brush my teeth. And you know I get up to pee at least once a night."

The bastard chuckled while he unlocked the cuff from the bed, but he left the metal bracelet dangling from her wrist. "You have five minutes."

She scrambled off the bed, her bare breasts bouncing as she scurried to the *en suite* bathroom, Dante close on her heels.

"Do you mind?" she asked before closing the door in his face, not waiting for his reply.

She sat down and buried her head in her hands, her head and heart at war with one another. She loved how she felt when she was with him—he made her feel alive. Beautiful. Desired. Protected. Loved... But she was only setting herself up for heartache—they were a lost cause.

"Three minutes," he announced from the other side of the door. She reached up and pushed the lock—not that it would really do her any good. It was a symbolic gesture, at best. She heard his chuckle at the sound of the click. "Oh, Kennedy Jones, you are adorable."

She wasn't adorable, she was a badass, and she needed to keep remembering that. Being in love with Mr. Sexy Alpha

Dante Mateo Guzman didn't lessen that. He was going to realize sooner or later that she was a force to be reckoned with.

****

Dante

"Ten, nine, eight..."

She opened the door just before he reached one. It was a good thing, although he had been hoping for a reason to put her over his knee, since she was still due for a punishment for her escape attempt.

"Can I brush my teeth, please?" she asked contritely. Too contritely. He nodded, not taking his eyes off her. She was up to something, he could feel it. Just like he'd felt it the night she left him after murdering his uncle. He wasn't necessarily fearful she'd harm him, but he was concerned she'd try another escape, and Dante wasn't letting that happen again.

He ran his hand over her ass, watching her tits jiggle in the mirror as she brushed her teeth. Fuck, he needed her. What did it say about their relationship that they'd seemed to connect again as they wrestled and fucked in the grass?

She set her toothbrush back in the cup, then looked at it for a moment before murmuring, "I can't believe you kept it."

"I knew you'd be back."

"I can't stay, Dante," she said in a quiet voice.

He tried to disguise his quick intake of breath. "Just give me a week, Bella. Let me make sure you don't have anything to worry about, then you'll be free to leave. If you still want to." He was going to do his damnedest to make sure she didn't want to.

"Okay."

"But I am going to have to punish you. That window is going to be a bitch to get repaired."

His cock got instantly hard when she stood on her tiptoes and whispered in his ear, "I deserve to be punished, Sir."

Now he knew something was *definitely* awry. He swatted her ass. "Get back in bed."

With a giggle reminiscent of Ruby Rhodes, she spun on the ball of her foot and headed back into the bedroom. He was on high alert when he followed her into the room.

When he attempted to hook the handcuff on the headboard, she jerked her wrist to her stomach and sat up straight.

"What the hell, Dante? I'm playing nice. I said I would give you a week. I understand it's in my best interest to stay put until you get things worked out with Ramon; there's no need for the handcuffs." She began to rub her wrist. "Take it off, it's making me itch."

He hesitated, taking a deep breath and looking up at the ceiling as he debated with himself about what to do.

He looked at her again—and found her with an annoyed expression on her face, the metal bracelet that had been attached to her wrist now dangling from the end of her fingertip.

"You do realize I'm trained to get out of these, right?"

God, he fucking loved her.

Chapter Fourteen

Kennedy

Dante smirked when he saw she'd slipped out of the cuff, and shook his head while he took the metal restraints from her.

Running his finger down her cheek, he growled, "Don't get too cocky, little one," then dipped his head and captured her mouth with his.

Kennedy whimpered as he pulled her against him. She'd been frightened when she saw him come out of the woods, but a tiny part of her had also been turned on. He was the only man to ever make her feel that he could not only handle her, but would protect her too.

She was a strong, independent, ass-kicking woman, and had lived her entire adult life not needing—or even really wanting—a man. Growing up with a mother who couldn't take care of anything by herself, relying on men for everything and always being disappointed by them, Keni had vowed that would never be her.

But something about Dante Guzman made her forget all about that whenever she was near him.

His arm came around her possessively, and she nestled into his side with a sigh and a smile.

"Goodnight, Bella," he murmured just before she fell into a peaceful slumber.

****

"Miss Ruby, you're back!" Rosa—one of Dante's pair of sweet, matronly housekeepers—exclaimed in surprise when Keni walked into the kitchen with the breakfast tray Dante had left for her in the bedroom.

She didn't suggest the woman call her Keni instead of Ruby; she didn't see the point.

"How are you beautiful ladies?" Kennedy asked in Spanish, being sure to include Maria, who was slicing vegetables but spoke limited English.

"Oh, your Spanish is getting better!"

When she had been here before as Ruby, Kennedy had often hung out in the kitchen. She had pretended to want the women to help her with her Spanish, but was secretly hoping to learn any gossip the help might dish on their employer, thinking she couldn't understand.

Not surprisingly, they never had anything but glowing things to say about Dante. They treated him like a son, and he was as good to them as their own sons were—probably better.

"I've spent the last seven months working really hard," was all she offered.

"Did you enjoy breakfast, Bella?" Dante asked, kissing her on the cheek as he walked into the kitchen and refilled his coffee mug. He'd once again made her breakfast. It wasn't exactly Rosa's cooking, but the fact that he'd done it for her made it delicious.

"I'm afraid I'm getting lazy, sleeping in and letting you make me breakfast. Why don't I make it tomorrow?"

He smiled as he spooned sugar into his coffee. "I'd like that."

"Would you mind if I used the gym and sat by the pool today?"

He eyed for her a beat as he tapped the spoon against the rim of his china cup. "Just be sure to sit under the umbrella with a hat. I wouldn't want your fair skin to get sunburned."

She knew it was more than that. It was probable that the property was under surveillance, and he didn't want her to be recognized.

"You know what? You're right. The sun is awfully strong this time of year, maybe I'll just sit on the enclosed porch."

He nodded in understanding and said, "I think that's a wise choice," then kissed her again before leaving. "Lunch at noon in the dining room?"

Her smile was for the benefit of the women watching them. She was starting to go stir crazy, but at least she was out of that tiny room and allowed to roam the estate. It was a start. And she'd probably feel a lot better after a workout.

"I look forward to it."

****

Dante

He walked into the dining room late for lunch. He'd been on the phone with Ramon, explaining—lying—about the plane having mechanical difficulties, which was why he'd sent John in his place last night. Fortunately, Laila had not minded. On the contrary, John had shown her 'a very good time.' Dante had summoned John to get the details, as well as his assistance supervising the men repairing the window and keeping them from being too curious about the room's contents.

"Good afternoon," he said, kissing Kennedy before he sat down. "John is arriving this evening, which means he'll be having dinner with us tonight. The workers are coming tomorrow morning"—he gave a dramatic pause with one eyebrow raised—"to repair the window. I want you to stay out of sight tomorrow until they leave."

She nodded her head thoughtfully.

"I need to go back to work soon," she announced as he laid his napkin across his lap.

He slowly creased the cloth across his legs before speaking. "Bella, we talked about this last night. You agreed to give me a week."

"I know, Dante. But I feel like my brain is turning to mush."

"It hasn't even been a week, little one. Do you not know how to relax?"

"I do, actually. But between not knowing what Ramon is going to decide, worrying about whether the agency is going to come looking for me, and not having any access to technology or a connection to the outside world, I'm a little on edge. Not to mention I have no idea what this 'punishment' you have in store for me is."

He leaned in to caress her cheek with his and was pleased when she closed her eyes in response. Kissing below her ear, he whispered, "I promise you'll like your punishment," then sat back in his chair. "I have to go to San Diego the day after tomorrow and meet with Ramon. But what if I give you some things to work on for me?"

She shot him a look before taking a sip of water. "I'm not helping you in your criminal activity, Dante."

Maria arrived with lunch so they fell silent until she left.

He began to cut his salad with a fork and knife. "I've told you, Bella, I'm working on legitimatizing our business. I'd only ask for your assistance with that aspect."

Dante wasn't blowing smoke up her ass. It was why he'd backed Ramon taking over as patrón. Ramon was younger, hungrier, and willing to listen to Dante's ideas not only on how to make the family syndicate grow, but also on legitimizing parts of it. Enrique had wanted to hear none of it; his attitude was, the way they'd done business had made them all very wealthy, so why change it?

It had become obvious that new leadership was necessary in the organization, and Enrique needed to be replaced—and eventually all that was left to determine was whether it would come at the hands of the CIA or from within the cartel itself.

Then his little assassin had shown up.

And he fucking fell in love with her.

Now more than ever he needed to turn more of the organization honest. Who better to help him than Kennedy? And she could marry him and have his children in the process. There was no downside to the plan—not that he could see. He knew he needed to proceed slowly, though.

She eyed him suspiciously. "What would I be doing?"

"Mostly consulting about security—both cyber and for the brick-and-mortar locations."

A small smile formed at the corner of her mouth. "Okay."

Seeing her happy made his heart swell and the rest of lunch was spent like most of their meals—discussing world events, pop culture, and politics. To test the waters, he mentioned an article he'd read about babies being exposed to technology too early.

"I don't want our kids being exposed to screen time until they're ten."

She pursed her lips at him. "That's incredibly unrealistic and will put them at a disadvantage. All their peers will have been operating technology since they were two."

But she didn't say anything about not having kids with him—as a matter of fact, she had pretty much conceded to having his babies.

"That's a good point." *See, baby? I'll compromise when it comes to our children.*

Chapter Fifteen

Kennedy

She sat in Dante's study, going over data for one of the several businesses the cartel owned. Dante said it was completely legitimate, although she had her suspicions about how much drug money was being laundered through it. But right now it was giving her some purpose, and she got to work alongside her sexy Latin lover.

Making out in the middle of a strategy session was definitely underrated.

Keni was straddling his lap, showing him the flaws in his system while he kissed her neck, when they heard, "Ahem."

Standing in the doorway with his knuckle to his mouth was John Turner, formerly known as Dr. Bruce Parker.

She decided to have a little fun at the men's expense.

"Dr. Parker! So nice to see you. How's the pediatric department doing these days?"

One corner of the handsome American's mouth turned up wryly, probably more to appease his boss than actual amusement at her remark. Dante smacked her ass in jest.

"Watch it, little one. You're already in enough trouble."

She rolled her eyes and kissed his cheek before climbing off his lap.

"I'll go check on dinner."

"Thank you. Let Rosa know we'll be ready in an hour."

She smirked as she walked past John in the doorway. He was definitely handsome, but nowhere near as gorgeous as Dante. "Good to see you again, John."

He nodded his head. "Ms. Templeton." It was the fictional name she'd given him on their run in Leavenworth.

She broke into a big grin. So she wasn't the only one who was going to be a smartass. She liked him already.

"How was the opera?"

It was his turn to smile broadly. "I definitely need to thank you for that."

"Sounds like there's a story..."

"Bella... Dinner." Dante's deep voice interrupted them.

She glanced at the man she'd been making out with all afternoon, doing his best to not appear annoyed that she and his henchman were behaving like old friends. If she weren't so happy that he'd given her something meaningful to do this afternoon, she might have considered poking the bear, just to be a brat. But she was probably in enough trouble as it was, so she simply smiled and said, "Oh, right. Let me go check on that," before disappearing into the kitchen.

Her handler would be beside himself if he knew that not only was she not going to attempt to covertly listen to Dante and John's conversation, she didn't even *want* to.

A tiny voice was whispering in her mind, "This is not good"—and her heart was telling the tiny voice to shut the fuck up.

*****

Dante

"You seem happy," John said with a grin as he sat down in the chair opposite Dante. "I haven't seen you this relaxed in a long time."

"I could say the same about you."

His right-hand man shrugged, trying to appear nonchalant, but gave up the act when he couldn't stop smiling.

"Best night of my life, man. I wasn't kidding when I said I need to thank her." He gestured to the doorway where Kennedy had disappeared.

If it were anyone but John, Dante would be put out at the thought of him thanking his Bella. But they had been friends since boarding school; there was no one Dante trusted more than him.

Still, he snarled possessively, "I'll pass it along for you."

That made his friend chuckle knowingly.

"So, what's the story? Does Ramon know she's here? I'm assuming the CIA does? Aren't you worried about a raid to come and get her—either from the US government or your uncle?"

"Ramon doesn't know she's here—or at least he didn't last night. She's made an appearance, though, since her little jailbreak, and I'm not sure how many of the staff have seen her and which ones are on Ramon's payroll as well as mine. She doesn't seem concerned about the agency coming for her, unless they think she's turned."

"Has she?"

He shook his head. "No, and I would never ask her to. It goes against who she is, and she'd eventually be miserable. It's one thing to ask her to overlook it, but it's completely different to ask her to play a role."

"So what were you two doing when I got here, other than acting like horny teenagers?"

"She was looking at some of the security plans for Emerald Woods."

Emerald Woods—one of their lawful businesses—owned marijuana dispensaries throughout the western United States. Profits were up and they were in the process of expanding, but security was a real concern.

"I can see how she'd be helpful with that."

"Wait till you get my bill." Kennedy was standing in the doorway with a smirk. "Dinner will be ready in an hour." She disappeared without another word.

John looked where she'd been standing, then turned back to Dante, shaking his head with a smile. "You're going to have your hands full with her."

The corners of Dante's mouth lifted in agreement. "Don't I know it."

He was looking forward to having his hands all over her later tonight, in fact—but right now, he needed to do something before dinner.

"Will you excuse me, John? I need to talk to Kennedy."

His friend grinned, assuming Dante was up to something. "Sure. I'll see you later."

****

He walked into his bedroom, bag in hand, and turned the lock after closing the door. Kennedy was sitting in lotus position on the king-size bed, going through the Wall Street Journal, which he still had delivered daily, Monday through Friday. Call him old-school, but he just liked the print version of that particular publication better than the electronic one.

She looked up at him and smiled as she turned a page.

With slow, deliberate steps, he approached the bed, and the smile fell from her face when she noticed his expression. She closed the newspaper and stared up at him with her emerald green eyes, not saying a word.

He knew his smile was menacing as he sat down on the edge of the bed and looked over at her—that was his intention.

She swallowed hard and squeaked out, "What's in the bag?"

"Part of your punishment, slut. Come here," and he pointed to a spot on the floor to the right of him.

She scrambled off the bed and stood where he indicated, her hands clasped in front of her. Her submissiveness was making his cock hard. He roughly turned her around and yanked her yoga pants to just below her ass, and squeezed her flesh with both hands.

"So fucking sexy," he groaned, then yanked her back so she stumbled toward him. He spun her around again and pushed her onto his lap, face on the bedspread, ass up.

Administering one smack, he commanded, "Count."

"One," she panted.

After five more blows, her creamy skin was a beautiful shade of pink. Gently rubbing her ass, he dipped his fingers between her legs, sliding a finger between her pussy lips. She was soaked.

Moving his finger in and out of her wet cunt, he admonished, "Little one, how am I supposed to punish you if you enjoy it?"

When he slid a second finger in, she arched her ass up, trying to provide him with easier access—he was somewhat limited, given the position of her yoga pants at the tops of her thighs.

"Such a greedy whore," he admonished, delivering repeated smacks to her dripping pussy with his wet fingers. She bit the comforter to keep from moaning.

He paused and pulled a bottle of lubricant from the bag, opening the top with a dramatic click. He tipped the bottle to pour it into her crack, and...

Nothing.

"Oh, for fuck's sake," Dante sighed, resting his elbow on her back as he twisted off the top. He pulled the foil seal off and threw it on the carpet. Her ass was shaking from her silent giggling.

"What's so funny?" he barked, then dispensed ten rapid blows back and forth. When he finished, her skin was red and she was panting.

Dante bent and kissed her warm cheeks before pulling them apart and pouring a generous amount of lube down her crack until it ran to her pussy. He slid a finger back inside her slick cunt and pressed one into her ass, and she was unable to control her moan.

"Such a dirty girl," he scolded, plunging his fingers deeper and faster. Kennedy's breathing became quicker, and he picked up the jeweled butt plug that lay next to the bag. Pushing it against her star until it breached her ring, he slipped it into her ass until just the sparkling diamonds on the end shimmered at him under the overhead lights. Yes, he'd bought a butt plug with real diamonds on the end. He was putting a diamond on her—or in her—one way or another.

Her pussy was drenched, and she was panting and grinding her hips against his hand when he smacked her ass and pulled her off his lap.

"You should go get cleaned up for dinner."

She seemed too stunned to even yell at him. All the times he'd been between her legs, he'd never stopped until she came—usually more than once.

The crime boss tugged her pants to her waist, then turned her around with a gentle swat on her butt and a small shove. "*Vamonos.*"

Finally, she found her voice and spun back around, glowering at him. "That's just mean."

"It's called *punishment* for a reason, Bella." He walked to where she stood, towering over her for a second before bending to whisper in her ear. "But I promise if you're a good girl, you'll be rewarded later. And don't you dare touch that pussy. No one touches that cunt but me, understand?"

He was about to make his exit, when she pointedly looked down at his crotch. He thought she was referring to his still-obvious erection.

"Baby, you have stuff on your pants."

He looked down and smiled. "Oh, thanks."

Whether it was Kennedy's pussy juices or the lube, or a combination, he wasn't sure. But as he changed out of them, he knew he was looking forward to getting this pair dirty too.

He paused in the doorway of the closet. "Oh, Bella?"

She looked at him through the mirror as she picked out an outfit for dinner.

"Wear a skirt and heels. No panties."

She pursed her lips and sassed, "Aren't you worried I'll accidentally flash John or one of the servants?"

He shook his head confidently and strode back toward her. "You won't. You wouldn't like the punishment if you did. But I definitely want you to flash me that pretty plug in your ass, so be creative, little one." With a kiss to her forehead, he whispered, "See you at dinner."

He stopped in the hall and adjusted his cock; he was hard again just thinking about it.

Chapter Sixteen

Kennedy
With her hands on her hips, she twisted to look over her shoulder at her ass in the mirror. There was something sparkling sticking out of it, alright.

She had diamonds shooting out her ass—*how glamorous is that?* she thought with a snort. Too bad they weren't multi-colored jewels; she'd feel like a unicorn.

Dante had inserted a butt plug in her bum, and she was supposed to walk down the stairs and have dinner with him and John like everything was normal, *and* find a way to flash the sexy bastard.

Keni wasn't sure if this was punishment for breaking the window and trying to escape or for talking to John. It wasn't like she was interested in John sexually, but she suspected Dante was reminding her who she belonged to.

Oh my god! I don't belong to anyone!

Still, she dressed in a skirt and heels, sans panties, as he instructed. As she spun around for one last look in the mirror, she realized she valued his approval of her.

How could she be so strong and independent—she was a damn assassin for the government, for Chrissake—yet still come completely undone with one touch from this man?

It had to be Stockholm syndrome.

But that doesn't explain the seven months you were apart from him and free. Why did you still want to be with him then? Because you love him.

Hey little voice, shut up.

Both men stood when she walked into the dining room. Dante's eyes shone with approval as he looked her up and down and held out her chair.

"You look beautiful, little one," he said, stroking her hip before she sat down. She knew he was checking for panty lines.

With a shy smile, she said, "Thank you."

Who was this woman? Was Ruby Rhodes more real than she cared to admit?

Setting the napkin in her lap, she looked at the guest across from her. "So, John, why did I never meet you when I was here before?"

"I was in Central America for a while, but I don't usually come to Ensenada anyway. I handle things in San Diego... and wherever else I'm needed."

"Like Leavenworth?" she smirked. "How long were you there?"

The handsome American darted his eyes to his boss, as if seeking guidance on how to answer.

"Long enough," Dante interjected.

Kennedy turned her attention to Dante. "I'm surprised you didn't come yourself."

With a knowing smile, he threw his arm around the back of her chair. "Who says I didn't?"

She narrowed her eyes. "I knew it! I knew you were there. I swear, I could sense you watching me."

He chuckled unapologetically and shrugged, saying nothing further.

Looking back at John, who was watching them closely, she asked, "So how long are you here for?"

"Just until the window gets fixed. I'll catch a ride to San Diego on D's plane the day after tomorrow."

Looking at the sexy Latino, she smiled. "Oh, that's right. You're going to the States. Think I could catch a ride, too?"

Dante gave a closed-mouth smile and patronizing wink. "Maybe next time, little one."

"I really need to feed my dog."

****

Dante

She was a regular comedienne. He knew damn well she would never keep a dog with her schedule, but he also knew she wanted one. Or at least Ruby had told him she did.

"Well, if you like, I can pick him up to bring back with me. Of course, you'll have to tell me where your place is…"

"Oh, I wouldn't dream of imposing on you like that—it's too far out of your way. It's fine. I'm certain my boyfriend has taken care of him by now."

Teasing or not, that shit wasn't funny.

Dante sat up straight and, with a clipped tone and a scowl, replied, "I can guarantee he has not, since he's sitting right next to you. Do you see a dog anywhere on the estate?"

Kennedy put her hand on his, knowing she'd woken the beast, and said softly, "You know I'm just teasing you, baby."

Her touch instantly soothed him, and he lifted her fingertips to his lips, murmuring, "I do." Then he softly squeezed her hand and growled, "But don't do it again."

As if trying to make amends, she blatantly dropped her spoon with an "Oops!"—not even attempting to be subtle—and bent over to pick it up, showing him that her ass still had the jeweled plug inserted in it. That brought an instant smile to his face and a thickening of his cock. His mood was back to mellow and content—how he'd been feeling since falling asleep with her in his arms last night.

Looking at the jewels winking at him under the dining room lights, he couldn't wait to have her back in his room, fucking her doggy style, and filling her up.

She placed the napkin back in her lap, and Dante leaned over to murmur in her ear, "Such a good girl. Good sluts get rewarded."

Keni turned her head to look at him directly, her eyes full of lust, and he couldn't help but gently kiss her right in front of John. She sighed against his lips when he slowly pulled away, resting his forehead against hers momentarily. He sat up straight just as Rosa entered with the first course on a serving cart.

Either his little assassin was giving him another Oscar-worthy performance, or she was on the verge of agreeing to stay with him. As always, time would tell.

Chapter Seventeen

Kennedy
Dante pulled her chair closer to his before dessert was served, keeping one arm around the back of her chair. He traced circles on the inside of her thighs while he and John talked shop as vaguely as they could in front of her.

She was still amped up from his orgasm denial earlier, but was paying attention to what they were saying. They were trying to speak in code—but doing a poor job of it—and she surprised the shit out of herself when she interjected, "That won't work."

Both men turned sharply to look at her.

Kennedy scowled and shook her head, ashamed of herself. But she continued, "They specifically look for that at border entry points."

Oh my god, what am I doing? I'm aiding criminal activity!

She stood abruptly. "I can't be here," she whispered and rushed out of the room.

Halfway up the enclosed servants' staircase, Dante caught up with her.

"Bella, wait," he said gruffly as he tugged on her elbow. The look of concern on his face when she turned around pulled on her heart strings. He offered a contrite smile, standing on the stair beneath hers so they were eye-level with each other. He tucked her hair behind her ear and kissed her wet eyes, then her cheeks and lips, ending at her forehead as he pulled her against him. "I'm sorry. I shouldn't have put you in that position."

The crime boss was apologizing to her. Dante Guzman never apologized to anyone.

"It's just a reminder of why I can't be here."

He leaned back to look into her face and stroke his fingertips along her cheek. "I'll do better, Bella. I promise."

This was more than a matter of *don't ask, don't tell*. Loving this man meant she was going against all her training and letting the government down. She should be doing surveillance and reporting back to the CIA, not helping him and his henchman avoid detection at the border and getting wet as she flashed him her bedazzled ass at the dinner table.

Kennedy owed her agency more, and she was going to do better.

"Okay," she whispered, giving him a small smile.

"Yeah?" he asked with raised eyebrows.

She simply nodded. Then he took her hand and escorted her to his bedroom. Whatever he was about to do to her, she'd do her best to not enjoy too much.

Good luck with that.

Shut up, tiny voice.

****

Dante

He didn't know if he believed her acquiescence—it seemed too easy, given how upset she was. He was on guard, paying close attention to how she behaved when he brought her back into his bedroom suite.

"You sure you're okay?" he asked, bending at the knee to be eye level with her. "I really fucked that up, Bella. I knew better, and I'm sorry."

"It's okay. Really."

Bullshit. Kennedy Jones should be handing him his ass for putting her in that position, but she wasn't. It was Ruby Rhodes who was standing before him, and he didn't like it. Ruby Rhodes was fake. She was also about to be punished.

Grabbing a handful of hair, he yanked her down to her knees.

"Ow, Dante! Fuck!"

There's my little assassin.

"Take my cock out, Ruby."

She moved to unbuckle his belt, then paused with her hand on the leather. Looking up at him, she whispered, "Why did you call me that?"

"Why are you behaving like her?"

Dropping her eyes, she tried to act offended. "I don't know what you're talking about."

He tilted her chin with his index finger. "No? Are you sure?"

Her only reply was the gentle shaking of her head.

He sat on the edge of the bed and patted his lap, and she scurried to lay across it with no further prompting. Dante flipped her skirt up and slowly removed the plug from her ass—they wouldn't be needing that now—then stroked her inner thighs using both hands.

"Well, then, let me tell you what I think is going on. I think you're back to pretending with me." She stiffened at his words, and he pulled on her biceps so she was sitting up next to him on the mattress. "I won't have it, little one."

"What do you want from me?" She leapt off the bed and began to pace in front of him. "I've told you I can't be with you, but you refuse to listen. You think somehow we can make it work, that love will conquer all, yet you insult me by discussing your criminal activities right in front of me—practically daring me to do something about it. I'm a fucking CIA agent, Dante. My job is to arrest you. You're making a mockery of my existence."

"I'm not making a mockery out of you. I just got too comfortable after working with you all afternoon on Emerald Woods. I told you I was sorry, Bella. I fucked up and put you in a position I never should have."

"I think you did it on purpose, to test me."

Did I?

Dante was silent for a moment as he pondered her accusation. When he finally spoke, it was low and quiet, and she stood at the corner of the bed, picking at a thread on the bedspread's stitching and listening without looking at him.

"If I did, it wasn't a conscious decision, but reflecting on the events of the evening, there may be some validity to your observation. The idea of you choosing me over your agency definitely has its appeal. To be honest, I was surprised when you helped me with Emerald Woods, so maybe my subconscious was trying to see how far I could push you. I've admitted several times now, it was too far. But don't you dare slip back into your role of Ruby Rhodes, thinking you can pretend with me again. It didn't work the first time, love, and it sure as fuck isn't going to now."

He stood and kissed her on the cheek. Kennedy finally looked at him with tears in her eyes.

"I'm so confused."

How could she still be confused? It seemed like the choice should be easy. If she loved him like he loved her, it would be.

"I'll leave you alone tonight to figure things out."

A look of panic came over her face, followed by resigned sadness.

"You're not coming back?"

The way she asked it—as if the idea not only upset her but hurt her—made him reconsider his decision to sleep in the guest room.

"No, I'll be back. But it will be late, and I'm sure you'll be asleep."

She looked down and skimmed the comforter with her fingertips, murmuring, "Oh. See you in the morning, then, I guess."

This time he didn't believe her vulnerability was an act, and he couldn't help but kiss her below her ear. She took a quick breath and he bit back a groan when he noticed her nipples pebbling under her blouse at his touch. Then she looked up at him with pleading green eyes, and it took every ounce of his willpower to walk out the door instead of wrapping his arms around her and sinking himself balls deep inside her pussy.

Chapter Eighteen

Kennedy
White teddy with no panties—check.

White thigh highs with lace garters—check.

Hair fluffed and makeup reapplied—check.

Perfume dabbed—check.

Sexy pose on the bed—check.

Now, she just had to wait for his return.

Keni was in love with Dante Guzman. There wasn't anything she could do about that but admit it, and there was no way she was going to turn him over to the CIA; she had come to terms with that, too. But she was leaving once Dante got Ramon's promise not to kill her. The agency was going to come looking for her sooner or later, and if they thought she was now working with Dante, she'd be dead, and so might he if she stayed. So, she was going to make amends with the cartel's money-man, enjoy what little time she had left with him, and look back on their time together with fondness. At this point, that was the best she could do if she wanted to keep everyone breathing. The memories were going to have to be enough, so she wasn't going to waste any more time. When Dante returned, she'd beg forgiveness and hopefully seduce him in the process.

At least that was the plan.

But as they say, the best laid plans often go awry.

Dante

He walked softly into the bedroom at two in the morning and stopped in his tracks at the sight in the glow of the bedside lamp.

There was his little assassin, fast asleep, looking like a Victoria's Secret angel, dressed in white satin and lace with her red hair fanned across her pillow. And no goddamn panties. She looked amazing—all that was missing were diamonds in her ass, and she'd be perfect.

What the hell was going on? Was this another ruse?

Truth be told, he was too fucking exhausted to analyze it. He stripped down to his boxer briefs, clicked the light off, and drew her body next to his before pulling the covers up around them. She whimpered incoherently as she rolled over and settled into his side, one hand on his chest, the other at his hip, inches from grazing his now-hard cock.

"Goodnight, Bella," he whispered against her hair.

"I love you, Dante," she mumbled, not opening her eyes but delicately rubbing her bare pussy against his thigh when she threw her leg over his.

Maybe he wasn't too exhausted after all.

"I love you, too, little one."

He ran his hand up her soft curves and palmed her left breast—then he heard her the soft whistle of her snoring.

Well, that settles that, he thought with a chuckle. He kept his hand on her supple mound and quickly followed her example.

****

He was having the most amazing sex dream—Kennedy's lips were wrapped around his cock with her warm hands tugging on his balls. It was fucking fantastic, and he was fighting against waking up. He didn't want it to end, but something was pulling him from his erotic slumber.

Dante felt her hair tickling his stomach and realized it wasn't a dream. Kennedy was slowly slurping up and down his hard-as-steel cock, stroking him from the base up.

He knew he should be suspicious as hell, but the way her tongue pressed against the underside of his prick made him not give a damn about anything else.

When he began to stroke her hair, she looked up at him and smiled with his dick in her mouth.

"Well, good morning," he smirked.

Pulling his cock out from between her lips, she continued jerking his shaft and cupping his balls, murmuring seductively, "Mmm, good morning. I'm sorry I missed you coming to bed last night," then dipped her mouth back on his cock and took him deep in her throat, rendering him temporarily speechless.

The wet noises she was making as she gargled with his tip were sexy as fuck, as was the sight of his cock buried between her lips. Dante began to make shallow thrusts further down her throat, and she stilled her movements, letting him fuck her face.

"Fuck, Kennedy!" he cried out, and held her cheeks in his hands while he plunged in and out. She ground her soaked pussy against his thigh and moaned, driving him over the edge to roar his release.

Even though she tried, she couldn't take everything he gave her, but the sight of his cum dribbling down her chin and onto her tits was pure porn.

"Oh my god, woman," he panted while she gently cleaned him with his discarded underwear. "What a fucking wake-up call."

Kennedy continued moving her hips in small circles on his thighs.

"I'm glad you liked that, baby. I wasn't sure if—"

He took the underwear, threw them on the floor, and pulled on her arm. Kennedy slid her body up to straddle his stomach, but he lifted her ass with both hands and moved her pussy to ride his face.

"Best damn breakfast ever," he growled, running his flat tongue up and down the length of her slit. Her soft moans and rocking hips soon rewarded his efforts, and he gripped her thighs, pulling her down onto his mouth to fuck her with his tongue, her juices coating his chin.

When he flicked his tongue rapidly over her clit, she cooed, "Oh my god, Dante, yes! Yes!" before falling forward, unable to maintain herself upright. He savored her taste as she moved her hips back and forth on his tongue while he delved deeper inside her. With his arms wrapped around her thighs to hold her still, he continued his assault on her cunt until she began to thrash above him as she reached her climax.

Her pussy now sensitive after her orgasm, Kennedy pushed him away, and he tugged on her waist so she was nestled on top of his chest with his arms wrapped her.

"Ruined," she sighed. "So ruined."

"You're damn right."

They were silent for a moment, then she quietly asked, "If we'd met in college, do you think things would be different?"

"Yes, I would have knocked you up and married you before you joined the Marines. We'd have four kids by now."

She lifted her head to look at his face, her brows furrowed. "I'm being serious. Would you... you know... would you still have chosen this life? In the cartel?"

He felt like there was a lot riding on his answer. Like this was a test of his character.

"Honestly, Bella, I don't know. I was a bit of a playboy in college, so I think if I had met you then, I wouldn't have been able to appreciate how perfect you are for me."

Her face fell.

Shit. Backtrack!

"But on the other hand, maybe if I had met you then, it would have woken me up. Maybe I'd have realized you were the one—like I did when I met you at forty—and married you and ended up on Wall Street."

"I don't like the cold."

That made him laugh out loud.

"Well, it's a good thing I ended up back in Ensenada then."

"Or we could have just picked somewhere warmer. But still legal."

He tucked her hair behind her ear.

"I could lie to you and say we're going completely legit, but I'd rather be honest with you. But I know I can't exactly do that either, given your current job. I don't know what the solution is, little one, but we will find it, because I can't be without you."

She rested her head back on his chest without responding, and they lay there in silence, each lost in their own thoughts while he gently stroked her hair.

To him, the solution was easy. She needed to quit the CIA, marry him, have his babies, and consult on the organization's legal businesses. And maybe their not-so-legal activities as well.

But the CIA would never allow it. So maybe the solution wasn't *that* easy.

Dante closed his eyes and pulled her closer. There had to be a way.

Chapter Nineteen

Kennedy

Once again, she hung out in Dante's office all day working on security options for the medical marijuana dispensaries. And, once again, she spent more time sitting on his lap than on the furniture in the room.

She hated how much she loved it.

He really was brilliant—his education was obviously not simply for show, and she might have fallen a little more in love with him as she watched him work. True to his word, they only discussed things that were legal, and when he had to take a phone call from his uncle, she left the room.

When she came back in, he looked up from his beautiful, ornate desk and smiled. "See, Bella? We can make this work. Just imagine our little ones playing in the corner."

If only.

The truth of the matter was he would be an excellent father. He was patient and never acted in anger, and when he'd explained the workings of Emerald Woods, he'd taken his time and ensured she understood everything she needed to know to help him.

And, yes, it had made her ovaries work overtime the night of her rescue mission when she'd seen him carry three-year-old Lucas to the room the boy shared with his stepmom, Cassie.

Lying in his arms that night, his cock still buried in her pussy after their last round of sex, she felt content, with sadness ebbing on that emotion. Their time together was going to be ending soon; they both knew it, although Dante did a good job of denying it.

"We belong together, little one," he murmured, breaking into her thoughts as if he'd read them.

He hadn't used a condom again, although he did ask her permission this time. She'd done the calculations in her head and felt confident she was not ovulating. The same could not be said for the night he'd taken her with the intention of getting her pregnant, and that worried her.

Another reason she needed to leave. Her period should be starting soon, and if it didn't, she was going to have decisions to make—without Dante's influence. Although, given her current employment status with the CIA, it wasn't really much of a decision. She couldn't exactly do covert ops with a baby growing inside her.

The thought made her sad, as did the idea of ending her time with her sexy Latin lover.

"We may belong together, but we can't be together."

"We'll figure out a way," he said confidently into her hair as he traced circles on her back, lulling her into a fitful sleep.

****

Dante

He had an ominous feeling when he woke up in the morning, even though Kennedy was still in his arms. He would be flying to San Diego with John, leaving his little assassin at the estate and trusting she'd be there when he returned. But he had a premonition she wouldn't be, and when he kissed her goodbye, he voiced it.

She looked him in the eye and promised, "I will be here when you return—hopefully with good news. You're right, we'll find a way to be together. I won't leave until we do."

Nonetheless, he was on edge for the entire plane ride to San Diego, checking the security feed often. It soothed his soul to see her working in his study or laughing with Rosa and Maria in the kitchen.

Walking into Ramon's office, his gut was still uneasy. Seeing El Rey, Miguel Hernandez, in a wingback chair smoking a cigar with his uncle didn't help matters.

The new Guzman *patrón* greeted him with a smile. "*Sobrino*! I'm glad you made it." He gestured to one of the chairs in the sitting area next to the men. "Please, sit down." Dante got situated, raising his hand with a subtle shake of his head at the proffered cigar. Ramon continued, saying with a raised eyebrow, "Miguel was just telling me what a great time Laila had at the opera the other night."

Dante had already told Ramon he didn't make it to San Diego the night of the opera, but apparently Laila had not told her father the same. *Well, shit. Now what?*

He was about to come clean with Miguel about John taking his place when Ramon interjected, "I'm glad you were able to show her such a nice evening, nephew. It meant a lot to Señor Hernandez to know his daughter was safe and in good hands. Safety of a man's loved ones is always the utmost priority, wouldn't you agree?"

Point received and taken, tío.

"I'm glad to hear she enjoyed it as much as I did," Dante said with as genuine a smile as he could muster.

The other man blew a smoke ring, then looked at his cigar and stated, "I understand you're taking her out again tonight."

He looked to Ramon for guidance. Dante wasn't exactly thrilled about lying to El Rey about who was actually dating his daughter. But Ramon only smiled sweetly at him, not offering any assistance out of this mess.

"I'm looking forward to it, sir."

Just then there was a knock on the office door, and John poked his head in without waiting for permission to enter.

"D, there's a situation that needs your attention, *now*."

He knew something was happening at his estate.

Ramon scowled, clearly offended, and demanded, "Can't it wait?"

Dante was already striding toward the door, but paused before walking out. "No, I'm sorry, it cannot," he said, then tipped his chin to the men. "It was nice seeing you, Miguel. Uncle, I'll be back in touch shortly."

The door hadn't even shut behind them before John thrust his phone into Dante's hands. The two watched the security camera feeds, horrified by the events unfolding in front of their eyes, as they made their way to the airport in record time.

Chapter Twenty

Kennedy
She was in the kitchen with the older housekeepers when she first heard the helicopters in the distance, and her hackles went up. As the sound got closer, Kennedy recognized the whirring of the blades on an Airbus 215.

"Into the pantry," she demanded and pushed the two frightened women inside. "Do not come out, no matter what," she said, then closed the door on their terrified faces.

Like a cat, Kennedy moved to the picture window to watch, confusion marring her face. The US government often used the Airbus 215, but the chopper setting down on Dante's manicured lawn did not look like anything she had ever seen her agency use. The men jumping out were dressed like they were part of the cartel, but she knew their flank formation by heart and identified the weapons they were carrying as being CIA-issued. The commands as they fanned out were given in Spanish, but not the Spanish of native speakers. They were too rehearsed, too proper—as if they had been learned in a classroom.

So just who the fuck was here to extract her?

Her strategy—whether to go peacefully or with a fight—was dependent on the answer.

So far, there hadn't been a firefight between Dante's security force and the men in the helicopter, which meant the men on the estate were expecting them.

Fuck. Too bad she didn't know how to access the panic room, short of climbing the outside wall and breaking the window again. The thought made her laugh, in an *I'm so screwed* kind of way.

She positioned herself in front of one of the cameras she knew about. If this was the handiwork of Ramon Guzman, hopefully Dante would recognize her abductors and be able to help her. If not, at least he'd know she had kept her promise and not left willingly.

The men breached the front door, and she put her hands up. She looked directly at the camera and mouthed *I love you* before a bag was thrown over her head, handcuffs placed on her wrists, and she was shoved out the door and into the waiting helicopter.

Her escape plan was already formulating in her head, but her impaired vision was posing a problem. She'd have to wait it out and see exactly whom she was dealing with.

Once they were airborne, she didn't have to wait long.

****

Dante

He felt as though his heart was being ripped from his body as he watched the men take her. They hadn't even gotten the jet in the air, and she was already gone.

"Take me back to my uncle's," he said calmly. Too calmly for all the pent-up frustration and rage coursing through his veins. Someone was going to die tonight if he didn't get her back unharmed—and it wasn't going to be him.

"We'll find her, D," John offered, a bravado and surety in his voice that Dante wasn't feeling. For the first time in as long as he could remember, he was scared. It was one thing to lose her because she didn't want to be with him—it was another thing entirely to lose her because she was dead.

"We have to, John. We have to."

"So what's the plan?"

He looked out the tinted car window and said matter-of-factly, "I put a gun to Ramon's head and pull the trigger if he doesn't tell me where she is."

John had been his friend for almost thirty years and knew better than to argue. He just jutted his bottom lip out and nodded. "Good plan."

"I swear to God, if they harm a hair on her head, I'm going to burn this fucking organization to the ground."

"Let's just focus on getting her back so that doesn't have to happen."

Dante's smile was humorless when he replied, "Always the voice of reason."

"It's why you pay me the big bucks, my friend."

Chapter Twenty-One

Kennedy
"Yeah, it's her... No, she was in the front room waiting... I'm fucking positive... Jesus. Hold on."

The hood was unceremoniously ripped off her head, and Kennedy blinked rapidly as her eyes adjusted to the light. A blond-haired man speaking perfect American English—probably from the East Coast, judging by his accent—was talking to someone on a cellphone. She glanced around and quickly confirmed her suspicions: They were on a ship. The man snapped a picture of her with his phone.

"Happy?" he growled into the receiver after sending the photo off.

She'd been able to deduce these were not Ramon's men, but if they were part of the agency, why was she still in handcuffs and not being given a hero's welcome home?

Her heart sank. This was a cleanup mission, and she was the mess. The CIA must think she was working with the cartel. Dante had a mole; there was no other explanation why they wouldn't have considered her a hostage.

Kennedy's mind raced trying to figure out who it could be. Maria? Rosa? She had a hard time buying it. Both women had worked for Dante's family since before he was born. Still, money was a powerful motivator, although she knew Dante took very good care of them and their families. Maybe it was

John? Again, that was hard to imagine—they'd been friends since boyhood, and the American seemed to have free rein in San Diego. Still, anything was possible.

At least her suspicions were confirmed: The agency wouldn't let her live if they thought she and Dante were together. *Yippee, I got it right... what does she win, Johnny? Oh, a bullet to the skull.*

Cue sad trombone music.

****

Dante

Miguel Hernandez's limo was leaving the gates as John and Dante roared up to his uncle's estate. It was probably just as well. Pulling a gun on El Rey would definitely be signing his own death warrant. He might survive killing his uncle if he couched it as revenge for Enrique's murder or as another coup, but taking down the head of some other family would mean outright war.

Besides, he seriously doubted Miguel knew anything about Kennedy or her whereabouts. Ramon, on the other hand, had better start talking fast.

He took the cement stairs to the front door two at a time, and didn't even bother ringing the bell. Instead he barged through the wooden double doors and marched straight to his uncle's office.

Ramon greeted him with a smile from behind his huge ebony hardwood desk. "Well, that was fast—everything okay? Quick thinking about Laila, by the way. Well done."

Dante drew his Glock from his waistband and pointed it at his uncle.

"Cut the shit, *tío*. Where the fuck is she?"

The look of surprise on the *patrón*'s face was unexpected. If he'd kidnapped Kennedy, he should have been anticipating this.

"I don't know to whom you're referring, but I'm going to assume it's your girl, and I can assure you, *mijo*, I am not behind whatever has happened."

The term of endearment caught him off-guard.

"But it was your men... your helicopter..."

His uncle shook his head. "*Órale*! Not my men. My helicopter is on the helipad on the roof—see for yourself."

Dante took his finger off the trigger and slid his pistol back into his waistband as he walked backward toward the door. Only once he'd cleared the threshold did he turn around and sprint to the stairs leading to the roof.

When he burst through the door, his whole body slumped forward at the sight of the chopper sitting there. It was like the fight had been knocked out of him and helplessness began to set in.

John was through the door seconds after Dante, and quickly came to the same conclusion as he looked at the occupied helipad.

"The CIA grabbed her."

"That's what it looks like."

"Why would they stage it to look like Ramon did it?"

He shrugged, though his mind was racing a million miles an hour. "Maybe to confuse my men so they didn't get in a gunfight. Or to confuse her."

Suddenly her words echoed in his head. *The agency would never let me live if I left to be with someone from the cartel.*

"We've got to find her, John. Get your ear to the ground and see if you can locate that helicopter. That'll be a good start."

"On it," his friend said, and disappeared out the door.

His uncle's voice interrupted his thoughts. "What do you need from me?"

"Find out how they knew she was there."

"Didn't the American woman and police sergeant know?"

"Yeah, but her agency only decided to come after her once she started helping me."

His uncle's eyes grew wide. "How was she helping you?"

Dante clenched his jaw, he'd already said too much. "Doesn't matter. Just find out who the leak is. I know you have some of my staff on your payroll, Ramon. Press them about what they know."

His uncle smirked with the realization that Dante knew about the spies, but paused in the doorway to the stairs. "I can't believe you're doing all this for a woman."

"Not just a woman. *The* woman. The one. Mine."

His uncle shook his head. He would obviously never understand; he was a playboy bachelor, uninterested in settling down. Just like Dante had been until a little over a year ago, before a feisty, beautiful redhead rocked his world. Maybe someone would do the same to Ramon someday; then he'd get it. Until then, Dante would have to rely on family loyalty to be the catalyst for his uncle's help.

The family loyalty card might be a little too bent to play at the moment.

He winced when he thought about pointing his gun at the head of the family. His father was going to have his ass when he found out how Dante had behaved—in his uncle's own home, no less.

"I'm sorry, *tío*. For the disrespect."

His uncle looked at him for a painstaking moment.

"I understand you're not exactly yourself right now. This is your one and only free pass."

Dante nodded humbly. "I appreciate your understanding."

Ramon smiled. "Let me go see what I can find out," he said, then disappeared, leaving Dante to crawl out of his skin with frustration and worry.

Chapter Twenty-Two

Kennedy

They hadn't put the hood back over her head. She was doing her best to appear small, unaware, and demure—definitely not a threat to these big, strapping agents. *Hehe.*

"It'd probably be frowned upon to have a little fun with her, huh?" she heard the broadest man there ask.

The one from the East Coast—who seemed to be in charge—laughed. "I wouldn't advise it. You might end up dickless."

"From her? Nah. I could take—I'd *like* to take her," the broad guy chuckled, laughing at his own perverted joke.

"Have you read her file?"

They lowered their voices so she couldn't make out everything they were saying, but she caught "handcuffed" and "bent over" and "desk." She traced a cuff with her index finger. If that asshole came near her, his friend's prediction of dickless was going to come true.

Just keep underestimating me. That was definitely a regular occurrence throughout her career, and one she used to her advantage whenever possible. Unfortunately, Mr. East Coast seemed to have done his homework on her and wasn't going to let his guard down as easily as the others. Probably the reason he was in charge.

East Coast's phone rang.

"Yeah?" he answered, then quickly cast a glance at her.

His face fell, along with her heart, but he quickly masked it, replying, "Yes, sir. I understand. That's an affirmative," then hanging up.

"Pull the anchor, we're moving," he commanded before heading above deck, and Pervy and the others in the room rose to attend to their tasks.

Her guess was they were never going to tell her about her impending death. It'd be quick; they'd take their pictures to confirm they'd completed their mission, then dump her body in the cold water. She looked around, trying to guess what she'd be weighted down with when they sank her to the ocean floor.

She caught Pervy watching her as the others exited the room, and gave him a seductive grin. Any agent worth his salt would know exactly what she was up to, but she was counting on him thinking with his dick. Hopefully it'd been a while since he last got laid.

Kennedy licked her lips and looked up at him through her lashes. The others were too busy preparing for launch to have noticed that their lecherous companion had not followed behind.

She leaned forward so her cleavage was on display.

"Do you think I could use the bathroom?"

The corners of his mouth turned up, and she saw the outline of his cock under his fatigues. If he wasn't going to kill her later, she might be impressed.

"Sure thing, sugar tits—I mean, Agent Jones."

He looked around to make sure no one was watching, then bent down to help her up from her seated position on the floor, feeling her up in the process. Her wrists were handcuffed in front of her, but she managed to stroke his cock through his pants while pressing into his touch and moaning softly.

He leaned over and ravaged her mouth with his, tweaking her nipple while she frantically rubbed his dick, making a show of not being able to do a good job with the shackles on. Not that she was going to need his help getting them off—it was all part of the vulnerable-girl illusion.

"Bathroom?" she panted against his lips. She needed to act fast before they were too far away from shore.

He slid his hand beneath her waistband and gruffly stuffed two fingers inside her pussy. Fortunately, she was wet. Her training had consisted of more than just slipping handcuffs.

"Oh, fuck, you aren't faking it, are you?"

"Of course not," she panted, grinding on his hand. "I'm so fucking hot for you."

He pulled on her arm with a meathead grin and escorted her out the door.

East Coast was walking back in as they did, his eyebrows raised and a frown on his face.

Pervy gestured his head toward her. "She's gotta go to the bathroom."

The leader was suspicious. *Smart man.*

"You sure you can handle her?"

Pervy waved him off. "I got this, Hughes."

She'd already slipped a cuff. He was gonna get it, all right.

Slipping the other, she kept her now-unrestrained hands in front of her as if she were still shackled. It'd been her experience that as long as she continued playing the part, no one realized anything until it was too late.

Pervy already had his cock out when he pushed her into the small bathroom, which barely fit one person, let alone two. She sat on the toilet and began to immediately stroke his thick shaft. It really was extraordinary, as far as dicks went.

"Mmm, let me suck your delicious cock, big boy," she cooed, dipping her head and running her tongue up and down his shaft. He bent his elbows and gripped the sink behind him when she deep-throated him, muttering, "Fuck, yesssss."

She slurped him up and down, then stopped, purring, "I want to ride you."

He quickly switched positions with her, anxious for her to sink her pussy down onto his shaft. He never saw the chokehold coming.

"This is what's going to happen next, stud. When you wake up, you're going to go to the deck and fire a round into the water. When everyone comes running, you're going to say I slipped a cuff and grabbed for your gun, so you shot me, and I fell overboard. I'll never resurface to refute your story, and you'll never come looking for me, and we'll both live a long, happy life. If you don't go with the story, or if you ever come looking for me, I will kill you. We both know I'm way better at this than you. Blink twice if you understand."

He blinked twice, and she finished rendering him unconscious.

Now for a brisk evening swim...

Chapter Twenty-Three

Dante

It was faster to take his uncle's helicopter back to Ensenada—he'd be on the ground in Mexico in the same amount of time it would take to drive to the airport from Ramon's estate. He and John were already in the air when they learned that the helicopter used to abduct Kennedy had been found near the marina. His most trusted men were ordered to scour the area and talk to anyone who might have seen anything—bribing or threatening them if necessary. Luckily Dante's name carried more clout than almost anyone else's in his seaside city, so people were willing to share what information they knew without much cajoling.

They'd learned a yacht had gotten a slip at the marina yesterday, but currently it was nowhere to be found. Witnesses said it had pulled up anchor less than an hour ago and hadn't returned. They also said the passengers were six males with athletic builds and short-cropped haircuts, in their twenties and thirties. They definitely fit the description.

He had choppers in the sky searching for the ship, although he knew that was like looking for a needle in a haystack. His attention needed to be on the leak in his home, which needed to be plugged.

"Eduardo, come in," he said in mock welcome as two guards hauled their coworker forward, one holding each arm.

The young man in their grip looked like he was about to soil himself. One of the men kidney-punched him, and he dropped to his knees.

Dante paced in front of him, his hands behind his back, expression pensive.

"Let's talk about this money that appeared in your bank account a few days ago. I know I didn't give you a bonus, and Ramon has confirmed he didn't give you a bonus. Last I checked, all your relatives are still alive, which rules out an inheritance. So..." Dante sat on the corner of his desk and spread his hands in a questioning manner. "Wherever could it have come from?"

"They threatened to kill my little girl," the man sobbed from his penitent position.

"Who?"

"I don't know—two Americans in mirrored aviators showed up at my house about six days ago offering me money. I refused, Mr. Guzman, I swear I did! But then they threatened my family... I just had to tell them when the woman got here—that was it. I swear I didn't tell them anything else."

"Not about how you found us on the lawn?"

"Well, I—" The kid's eyes darted around the room, as if looking for an escape. "I might have mentioned that's how I knew she was here."

Dante nodded knowingly, saying nothing further.

Eduardo sniveled, "Are you going to kill me?"

The estate owner opened his mouth, then closed it again with a grimace. After a minute, he answered truthfully. "I don't know."

"I've got a daughter," the man said, weeping openly. "She's two."

Goddammit, this was why he wasn't involved on this end of things. He didn't have the stomach for it. Money, assets, spreadsheets, strategies—that was his forte, not this shit.

Still, Kennedy was missing because of this man's betrayal.

With a menacing tone, Dante declared, "You better hope I find my Bella alive and well. If I don't... your headless corpse will be hanging from a bridge."

"I didn't want anything bad to happen to her! I thought she'd be safe here. I thought she'd be protected."

Those words were like a knife to his stomach. He should have been here to protect her.

"Get him out of here," Dante snarled. The guards dragged Eduardo from his office, not even letting the man regain his footing.

"We'll find her, D," John said softly from his position on the couch.

"I know," he replied with a sigh, running his fingers through his hair before pouring a glass of whiskey. *But is she going to be alive when we do?*

"The yacht is back in the marina," John said, looking at a text on his phone. "Six men got off; no sign of her."

"Are they the men in the security footage?"

He could tell John was warring with what to say.

Dante sighed, slamming his whiskey tumbler down a little harder than he'd intended.

"Just fucking tell me. I know you want to protect me, but give it to me straight. You're the one person I can always rely on to do that."

John took a deep breath. "From the pictures Hector just sent, I would say yes."

With a sweep of his arm, the contents of his desk went flying across the room. The sound of his whiskey glass shattering against the wall blended with his roar of anguish and rage as his papers slowly floated to the floor.

"Dante, how many times did you underestimate her, only to have her hand you your ass? And you know her. I'll bet anything these men did the same thing, and she escaped."

His gut was telling him she was alive, but he was worried it was just wishful thinking.

"Have them do an air sweep of the water five square miles from the marina," he ordered quietly, not looking at his friend. "One hundred thousand dollars to whoever finds her."

He wouldn't rest until he found her—dead or alive.

****

Kennedy

The ship wasn't far from shore when she dove overboard. Still, the cold water made the swim back to land exhausting, and she collapsed on the sand, overcome with fatigue.

Keni was unsure what time it was when she woke, but it felt like the middle of the night. She needed to find a place to hole up and plan her next move.

Chapter Twenty-Four

Dante

It'd been twenty-one agonizing days since Kennedy was taken from him, and he'd been a bear to be around ever since. The constant stream of liquor that had been coursing through his blood for three weeks straight probably wasn't helping things.

Eduardo was still alive, but only because Dante believed ordering his death was like conceding she was dead, and he just couldn't accept that. It didn't mean the young man wasn't made an example of what happened to those who betrayed the Guzmans—he probably wished he was dead. Still, getting your ass beat was a far cry better than sitting in a vat of acid, which was what Ramon had suggested.

John had been a good friend. He had stayed in Ensenada most nights, flying back and forth to San Diego to attend to business in the States and, Dante suspected, squeeze in time to see Laila when he could. Good for Turner. If anybody deserved happiness, it was his oldest and best friend.

Sleep eluded the Mexican most of the time, so he was either inebriated or beyond exhausted when he would finally make his way to his room, oftentimes choosing to sleep on the leather couch in his den instead. Being in his big bed without her next to him was painful. He hadn't allowed Rosa or Maria to change the sheets, and he could still catch her scent on them sometimes. He savored that.

It was well after midnight—again—and the two men were in Dante's office. John never complained, no matter how late Dante kept him up, although he suspected his friend was exhausted tonight. John tried to stifle a yawn.

"I'm sorry, *mi amigo*. Go to bed," he apologetically ordered.

"Nah, I'm fine."

"No, I'm going to turn in too. We've got a big day tomorrow, I've got the conference call about the dispensary permits, and then I need to get with the builder."

He shut the lights off in the den, and they made their way to the stairs.

Outside the guest suite, John said, "Why don't you let me handle the builder, D?"

Dante clutched his friend's shoulder with gratitude.

"Because you've got enough to deal with, and I need to keep busy or I'm going to lose my mind."

"Understood. I'll see you in the morning."

John closed the suite's door, and with a heavy sigh, Dante started toward his room. He stood outside in the hall, gathering the mettle to go into the master suite. He both loved being in there and hated it—everything reminded him of her.

Taking a deep breath with his eyes closed, he pushed the door open and stepped inside. His heart skipped a beat at the obvious lump under his covers, and he approached cautiously, his gun drawn.

It was Kennedy's delicate face peeking out from the blankets. He set his gun on the nightstand, blinking several times in case his eyes were deceiving him; then, gathering her in his arms, he sent a silent prayer of thanks to the man above.

****

Kennedy

She'd slipped into the house undetected during security's eleven o'clock shift change, and snuck into Dante's room. There she proceeded to strip naked and nestle into his high-thread-count sheets and cozy comforter.

The last three weeks had been spent in a constant state of alert, never sleeping for more than a few hours—and only when she could hole up somewhere she felt safe enough doing so. Immediately returning to the estate after she dove off the deck of the yacht wasn't an option. She wasn't sure if Pervy would follow her orders—perhaps he had even been discovered unconscious before he'd been able to do as she'd instructed. Kennedy knew she couldn't chance going back to the estate right away, although she desperately wanted to reach out to Dante and let him know she was all right. But doing so was too risky.

She'd cut her hair and dyed it brown. It wasn't much in terms of a disguise, but she didn't have the resources for more than that. She would make it back to her little cabin in Arizona to retrieve her money and personal effects when the dust settled, but in the meantime, she was surviving on what she could steal or borrow. While she was confident no one knew about her little place tucked away in the mountains near the old mining town of Bisbee, crossing the border would be difficult—especially as locked down as it had become with the migrant caravans from Central America headed to the US. She wasn't taking any chances—not when her former employer wanted her dead. She was safer in Mexico, for now.

It wasn't until she read her obituary on the website of Fargo's daily newspaper, *The Forum of Fargo-Moorhead*, that she felt it was safe enough to return to Dante's. She'd need to figure out a way to contact her mother and Reagan someday, but it was probably for the best if they thought she was dead. They'd be in less danger that way.

Being on the estate—with Dante's security on patrol and Dante himself here—Kennedy finally let her guard down and burrowed into the thousand-dollar linens. She fell into a long-overdue slumber while waiting for the man she loved to come to his bedroom and discover her.

The familiar scent of Dante's cologne filled her senses, and she felt her body being lifted and manipulated until she was in his lap, wrapped in his huge embrace with the bedding still half around her. His strong hand held the back of her head as he kissed her hair and whispered, "My dear, sweet Bella, thank god you're alive," while gently rocking her.

Clinging to him, she murmured, "I'm so sorry you were worried."

He pulled away to look at her face, staring at her in wonderment, then pulled her back against his chest.

"I can't believe you're here. If I'm dreaming, don't wake me."

With an exhale, he laid her out in the bed, fixing the linens around her, then stood and stripped down to his black boxer briefs before sliding in beside her. Once again, she was in his arms, and the skin-to-skin contact made her break out in goosebumps.

"I love you, Kennedy Alicia Jones," he sighed.

She stroked the hair on his chest.

"I love you too, Dante Mateo Guzman. I'm back forever."

Her words seemed to settle his soul, and soon they were both fast asleep.

Chapter Twenty-Five

Dante

He opened his eyes to the morning sun filling his room. Judging by the brightness of the light coming through the windows, it was already mid-morning. He'd slept better than he had in weeks—three weeks, to be exact. Kennedy was still in his arms; it hadn't been a dream. But how? How was she here?

At the moment, Dante didn't care. He'd find out the how soon enough.

Watching her sleep, he realized she'd cut and dyed her hair. He preferred her long, naturally red hair—but he didn't care if she was bald, as long as she was in his bed again.

Her face looked gaunt, and his soul ached at the thought of what she'd had to endure over the last three weeks. The fact that she was lying next to him proved what a badass she really was, and he'd never make the mistake of underestimating her again. He'd also never make the mistake of leaving her alone again.

As if sensing she was being stared at, her eyes fluttered open, and she greeted him with a bright smile when she found him watching her.

"Good morning," she said softly.

"Yes, it is."

"Have you been awake long?"

"No, I slept like the dead, since I was finally able to breathe again. Ironic, I know."

Her lips turned up in a closed-mouth grin.

"I completely understand."

"Do you want me to bring breakfast up here, or should we go downstairs together?"

She shook her head. "You have a mole, Dante. That's got to be how the CIA knew I was here willingly, which is why they want me dead. I need to stay hidden."

"I know. I've taken care of it."

"You do? Who was it? It wasn't Rosa or Maria, was it?"

The idea made him laugh. Those two women had doted on him his entire life. The chances of one of them betraying him were as good as his own mother doing so, if she were still alive.

"No, it was Eduardo, and he has been dealt with."

Kennedy grimaced. "Aw, Eduardo? I know he had a little girl. Rosa and Maria were always bringing in frilly baby outfits for her. I hope you're going to make sure she's taken care of. You know the CIA isn't going to."

"I didn't kill him."

She cocked her head in surprise. "No?"

"No. I think letting him live may come in handy down the road, should the CIA come knocking on his door again. There's no way they'll think he's been discovered if he's still alive to tell about it, so they might try their luck with him again."

"That's pretty smart, actually."

Dante smirked. "You know Stanford doesn't just give those MBAs away, right?"

Keni rolled her eyes. "Somehow I don't think *Cartel Strategy 101* is on Stanford's curriculum."

His smirk turned into a smile, and he winked. "Good point. But!" He held up his index finger. "Personnel Management is, and it's the same concept."

Leaning over to kiss his cheek, she cooed, "The brilliant Stanford grad."

He slid his arm around her middle and pulled her closer just as her stomach rumbled loudly. He chuckled, and she giggled, saying, "I guess I'm a little hungry."

Dante kissed her hair. "When was the last time you ate, Bella?"

"Hmm..." She furrowed her brows as she considered his question. "I grabbed a croissant off the counter last night when I snuck in."

"And before that?" He pulled her out of bed, admiring her naked body before handing her a robe.

She put it on, but hesitated before answering his question, as if she had to think about it.

"I don't really know. The last three weeks have been an exercise in staying out of sight as much as possible while trying to stay alive."

"You should have come here. I would have taken care of you."

"I couldn't risk it."

"I've doubled my security staff—"

"I noticed that, yet I was still able to sneak inside last night. You need to make some improvements," she scolded.

They started down the stairs to the kitchen.

"Why don't you work on that later with José, the head of security?"

Before she could respond, Rosa and Maria were hugging her.

"Oh, Miss Ruby! You're okay! We've been so worried!"

Dante knew Kennedy had shoved the women into the pantry the afternoon the CIA came for her, in an attempt to keep them out of harm's way. The two *abuelas* had been beside themselves with worry ever since, asking him for updates daily. He'd started to avoid them; he hated having to say out loud every day that there was no word on her whereabouts, or even if she was still alive.

"Ladies, her name is actually Kennedy, but we're probably going to have to change that."

Keni gave a melancholy smile and a big sigh.

"I hadn't thought of that, but you're probably right. Any ideas for a new name?"

To him it was obvious.

"Bella, of course." Then with a raised eyebrow, he added, "Guzman."

She snorted. "I guess I can make up any name, I want, huh?"

He had to fight to keep the growl from escaping his throat as he told her, "You're marrying me for real."

Kennedy patted his cheek as she walked toward the orange juice and coffee carafes on the kitchen table.

"You really need to work on your proposal skills, Stanford grad."

He caught her by the waist, spinning her around and dipping her before planting a kiss on her mouth.

"I'll take that under advisement," he murmured against her lips with a small smile before standing her upright and pulling out her chair for her.

Just then John walked in. His eyes widened when he caught sight of her, and he broke out into a wide grin.

"Sonni Templeton! It's about damn time you showed up."

This confused Rosa.

"Wait—I thought her name was Ruby, but it's really Kennedy, yet she's going to go by Bella Guzman, and now you're saying a completely different name."

Dante kissed the sweet lady's cheek. "It's an inside joke, *bonita*. She's Bella from now on."

He sat down across from Keni and, using his foot, pushed out the chair on the end for John.

"So," his best friend said as he sat down. "What the hell happened?"

****

Kennedy/Bella

She didn't get too graphic as she told the story of how she escaped. She left out the part about her mouth being on Pervy's genitals. Dante would understand—although it would hurt him—but it wasn't necessary to the story; Rosa, Maria, and John definitely didn't need to know, so she omitted it. Instead, she focused on the exhausting swim to shore and how she'd managed to remain hidden for the last three weeks.

"I really need a professional cut and color," she lamented while examining the ends of the crudely chopped and mousy brown strands between her middle and ring fingers.

"I can have my stylist come to the house," Dante suggested.

Kennedy pressed her lips together to keep from teasing him about having a stylist, but John picked up that ball and ran with it.

"Did you just say you have a fucking *stylist*?"

Dante furrowed his brow. "Yeah. Why?"

"A stylist?"

"Who the fuck cuts *your* hair?"

"Well, since I have a set of balls, I go to a barber."

The Mexican made a show of rolling his eyes.

"Americans. So insecure with their masculinity."

John chortled and took a sip of coffee. "Whatever, dude. You have a stylist."

Kennedy interjected. "Well, I would love for your stylist to come do my hair, so if you could arrange that, I'd be ever so appreciative."

The corner of his mouth lifted. "How appreciative?"

Her smirk matched his.

"I just told you. Ever so appreciative."

He leaned back, nonchalantly throwing his arm along the back of the chair next to him with a twinkle in his eye.

"You can do better than that, Bella."

Maria set a plate of pancakes in front of Keni, and her mouth began to water from the smell alone. She was ravenous but trying to be polite and not inhale her breakfast, like she had done as a kid on Monday mornings at school, after going all weekend without eating.

"I'll show you how grateful after breakfast," she teased.

"Trying to eat here," John said obnoxiously as he shoveled a forkful of omelet into his mouth.

With as much restraint as she could muster, she took her time buttering her pancakes before pouring syrup over them and taking a glorious bite.

She closed her eyes, savoring the taste. "Best breakfast ever, Maria," Kennedy called—in Spanish so the woman could understand her compliment.

That brought a smile to the older woman's face, and she cupped Kennedy's cheek in adoration after she set Dante's breakfast on the table in front of him.

"Estamos tan contentos de que hayas vuelto, mija."

"I'm glad to be back," Kennedy responded, kissing Maria's knuckles as she affectionately squeezed the woman's hand.

She *was* glad to be back. This was the one place Kennedy had ever felt like she was truly home—although she conceded that was probably going to change. She would no longer have free rein to roam and come and go as she pleased, as she had when she was playing the part of Ruby Rhodes.

Freedom was a beautiful thing, and she was going to miss it. But being safe and with Dante was worth it.

Chapter Twenty-Six

Kennedy/Bella

She was standing at the kitchen island, laughing with the two housekeepers, when she glanced over at Dante at the table and noticed him watching her with a thoughtful smile.

When she returned his smile, his face changed. Kennedy knew what the look in his eye meant, and it made her toes curl with excitement. He never failed to make her feel desirable, like she was the only woman on earth he wanted.

Sliding his chair out, he stood and sauntered toward her with a knowing smirk, offering her his hand.

"If you'll excuse us, ladies, we have a lot we need to get done today."

Kennedy took his hand, allowing him to escort her out the door.

"First, I'm going to make love to you, then I'm going to fuck you rough and hard," he whispered in her ear as they ascended the stairs.

"Can't we do that in reverse?"

She peeked over her shoulder to gauge his reaction, and found him with a lopsided grin.

"Yeah, we can do that," he said with a chuckle.

"Good."

They reached the bedroom, and his hand came around the back of her neck to guide her through the door. Once inside, the door slammed shut when he shoved her body against it. One of his hands was around her throat while the other untied her robe and yanked it open to expose her naked body to him. He palmed her tits, kneading the flesh before tweaking her nipples. The pain was brief before turning to pleasure that shot straight to her pussy.

Kennedy tugged on his robe, opening it as his mouth enveloped hers in a frantic kiss. She began to grind shamelessly against his boxer briefs and the hard cock underneath them.

Tugging on her hair, he panted against her neck, "On the bed—on all fours, ass up. Now," then sank two digits inside her soaked pussy.

Um... now? Can't we wait a minute? She tilted her head back against the varnished wood as the feeling of being pleasured overwhelmed her senses.

He moved his thumb in circles over her clit, hissing, "*Now*, Bella."

This was a test of her willpower, and she was failing miserably. She didn't care—as long as he kept fingering her.

"Spread your pussy," he demanded.

Kennedy immediately complied, widening her stance as she leaned against the mahogany door, and pulling herself apart. Dante delivered repeated slaps to her clit, making her moan. He chuckled, "It's impossible to punish you, little one. You like it too much. Your cunt is getting wetter."

He curled his finger inside her pussy, making a *come here* motion as he hit her G-spot, while polishing her nub with his other hand. She began to tense, and he increased his tempo to a frenzied pace until she fell against his chest while the orgasm ripped through her.

"You sexy fucking bitch, you just squirted all over my hand."

Sorry, not sorry.

Pulling his fingers from inside her, he slid them into her mouth for her to taste herself. "On the bed, on your fucking knees, now," he growled.

She scampered to the mattress and quickly got into position—head down, ass up. He pulled on her hips, dragging her to the very edge of the bed so he could slam his cock deep inside her drenched pussy while he remained standing. He didn't even give her any time to get used to his size, immediately relentless with his thrusting. The sound of slapping skin filled the room, along with her whimpers and his grunting.

The guttural noise coming from him was almost feral, and he was pounding her like a beast possessed. His balls smacked her sensitive clit every time he plunged inside her heat, and along with his sexy growling, it sent her into another orgasm. Crying out his name as she went over the edge, her pussy milked his thrusting cock, which didn't miss a beat. His groans became shorter and faster, his fingertips tightened on her hips, and his rhythm became erratic as he emptied himself inside her. Dante bent over and leaned onto her back, his arms reaching around to palm her tits and briefly tug her closer to him.

"Fuck, Bella," he panted as he rolled onto his back. Reaching over, he pulled her on top of him, and she burrowed her face into his neck.

Their hearts felt like they were pounding in time with each other, even slowing at the same pace until their breathing evened out.

"I'm sorry, Kennedy," he said softly.

She lifted her head, wrinkling her brows in confusion.

"I didn't use a condom, and I didn't pull out. I should have asked you. I know you don't want to get pregnant yet."

This was her opening.

"Too late," she whispered in his ear.

****

Dante

What the fuck did she just say?

He held her chin between his thumb and knuckle of his index finger.

"What did you just say?"

God, he didn't want to get his hopes up in case he had misunderstood her.

"We're having a baby."

Dante moved his hand from her chin to clutch her biceps.

Holy fucking shit.

HOLY FUCKING SHIT.

"Are you sure?" He still didn't want to give himself false hope.

"I took a test yesterday morning."

He tried to dampen his elation and keep the smile from his face as he somberly asked, "Are you okay? I know this isn't what you want."

She seemed offended, and curtly replied, "I never said I didn't want a baby. I just didn't see how I could have one with you or while working for the CIA."

"And now?"

"Well, since my agency tried to kill me, I think it's safe to say I'm not going back there. And since I'm hoping they think I'm dead, I guess as long as I stay in disguise and keep a low profile around here, it'll be okay. I'll just need to figure out how to reconcile your cartel activities with my conscience."

"We need to get your new identity documents, stat, so I can marry you."

She bit her bottom lip.

"I know it's silly, and it's just a name, but do you think we could have two sets of paperwork? I want one with my real name, even if it just sits in your safe. I want it to be real, you know? The second set with my fake name can be recorded, but I want one to be with my legal name, too—even if it's just for my records."

"Bella, we can have five sets, as long as you're married to me on each one."

"And another thing... I think we should wait at least another six weeks to tell anyone about the baby, when the chance of miscarriage has lessened."

Dammit, he wanted to shout it from the rooftops, right now! But he understood her concern.

"Okay," he agreed. "But I have to tell John. He's gotten me through these last three weeks; it seems only fair to share my good news with him. In confidence, of course. He won't say a word; he's like a vault when it comes to secrets."

"How did you survive when he was in Central America?" she teased

"I fell in love with you," he grinned.

Kennedy felt a little jealous and realized she missed her sister more than ever. "He's like your brother."

"More than my biological brother. I'd trust John with my life. I have, actually, on more than one occasion."

She cocked her head. "How long have you been friends?"

"Since I saved him from getting beat up when we were twelve years old in boarding school."

He chuckled at the memory of his then-scrawny friend raising his fists as older boys descended on him for being a smartass. Dante had come to his rescue, and the two had been inseparable ever since. Throughout their youth, John had more than returned the ass-saving favor, and they'd remained close through college, even sharing an apartment. John had attended MIT in Boston, while Dante studied at Boston College. The American had gone into the private sector, making a nice living as an engineer in Silicon Valley, while the cartel leader's son went to Stanford. When Dante had decided to go into the family business, there was no one else he wanted as his right-hand man. He'd carefully broached the subject with his best friend, who, after three years of being chained to a desk, didn't need much convincing to say yes.

Thank God, because there was no one he trusted more than John.

Now they were starting a new chapter in their lives, one that included a wife and children—at least for Dante, although he wouldn't be surprised to learn the American wasn't far behind. Laila Hernandez seemed to be occupying a lot of his time. The idea of having a target on their backs took on a whole new meaning. Granted, Kennedy could hold her own, but what about their kids? What about Laila? She seemed a little more fragile than his Bella—probably the result of being a crime boss' daughter, and being sheltered most of her life to keep her safe.

Kennedy pressed her lips against his, bringing him back to the present.

"What are you thinking about?"

He brushed her bangs across her forehead.

"What I'm going to do if we have a little girl. I'll want her to be a badass like her mom, but I worry that I'm going to want to protect her too much for that to happen."

She gave a sad smile. "I worry about that, too. I wish we could just go somewhere and live a normal life—away from the cartel, the CIA, everything."

Unfortunately, they were going to need the cartel's money to remain safe, so that wasn't an option for them. Still, maybe they could make some compromises regarding the normalcy she desired. Her next words, however, made him think she wasn't sure what she desired right now.

"But what do I know about normal? Nothing about my life has been normal so far."

Kissing her cheek, he whispered, "We'll figure it out together, Bella."

Chapter Twenty-Seven

Kennedy/Bella

She hadn't been surprised when the two pink lines had appeared on the stick she peed on—she'd been feeling nauseous for the last few days, along with being more exhausted than she'd ever been before. The missed period was also an indicator, but that happened to her a lot when she was in the field. Kennedy had always assumed it was just a defense mechanism her body employed, but it had felt different this time. Coupled with the unprotected sex she and Dante had around the time she thought she was ovulating, she had accepted becoming a mother before she even took the test.

It was an odd feeling. She'd spent so much time focusing on why she couldn't have a baby, but now that those reasons were no longer a factor she realized she was actually happy with the idea. Although when she had taken the test, she'd been scared to death, considering she was in a pharmacy bathroom in Ensenada, taking a pregnancy test she'd had to steal. What little money she'd begged—spinning a sob story for cruise-ship tourists on a day trip in Ensenada—had gone toward seedy hotel rooms where no questions were asked, where she could hide out from the people who wanted her dead.

Feelings of nervousness were also pervasive. How could they not be? She hadn't exactly had the ideal role model when it came to motherhood. She and her little sister had managed to turn out okay though, so maybe her kid wasn't completely doomed. Not to mention Dante seemed to have had the perfect childhood, even if it had been spent in boarding schools when he grew older.

"I don't want our kids to go to boarding school," she announced as she walked in the bathroom as he was toweling off from his shower.

Wrapping the towel around his waist, he nodded thoughtfully but chuckled when he replied, "Okay. I don't have a problem with that. How do you feel about nannies and tutors?"

"I'm all for both—in moderation."

But there was a bigger issue at stake, one she was worried they weren't going to agree on.

"I want the baby to be born in the US, Dante. I don't want citizenship to ever be an issue. And I think we should raise him there. We both know the educational system is better in America." *At least he should know, considering he was schooled in the States.*

With his eyebrows raised, he smirked, "*Him*, huh?"

She shrugged. "I don't know, maybe. It's better than saying *it*. You're not answering the more important questions."

"We've got plenty of time to worry about this, Bella."

That was the equivalent of her mom saying, "We'll see." And just like when she was little, that answer wasn't acceptable.

"We really don't. It's not like we can just move anywhere without a lot of research and planning taking place. Where we end up is going to take a lot of preparation."

He rubbed the back of his neck—something he only did when he was upset. *Why is he upset?*

"Kennedy, that's number seventy-six on the list of a hundred things we need to worry about right now."

Maybe it was the last three weeks catching up with her, or maybe it was her pregnancy hormones—or a combination of both—but she stubbornly refused to drop it. She crossed her arms across her chest.

"I disagree. I think this is far more important than number... whatever you said."

"Bella, we'll talk about this later."

"I want to talk about it *now*." She had been dangerously close to stomping her foot, but caught herself.

Dante started toward his closet.

"Unfortunately, I can't talk about it now, I have conference call about the new dispensary permits, and then another phone meeting with the builder we've chosen."

She followed him into his closet, tears starting to well up in her eyes at his lack of consideration—which was bullshit. She had never been a crier before. Ever. If this was a preview of her next eight months, she was going to have to take a hard pass on this hormonal crap.

"Well, we're talking about this later tonight. I want it resolved before we go to bed."

He studied her through his mirror as he buttoned his shirt, not saying anything. When he'd pulled his jacket on, he turned around and kissed her cheek.

"Fine. We'll talk about this at dinner, little one. Do you feel up to sitting in on this conference call about the permits?"

She shook her head. "I haven't even showered yet, and I'm feeling kind of tired."

He smiled knowingly. "Why don't you get some rest. We'll have lunch with John when you get up and around. You're welcome to come down to the study anytime if you feel up to it; if not, no worries. I just want you to take it easy. Our baby has been through a lot already."

That was true. If she went full-term with this kid, she could guarantee he was going to be a fighter.

Kennedy stifled a yawn as she followed him back into the sleeping area of the suite, and he smiled lovingly at her while pulling back the bedding.

"Go back to sleep, Bella. Take care of yourself and our baby."

She snuggled into bed, and he kissed her cheek again before tucking her back in.

"I love you, little one."

She was suddenly too tired to even respond, and soon fell into a dreamless sleep.

****

Dante

John was sitting on the couch in Dante's office and smiled big when the Mexican walked into the room.

"Congratulations, man. I told you she escaped from those bastards."

Dante shook his head in disbelief. "I still don't know she did it. She is definitely a force to be reckoned with." He paused, then continued, "And she's going to be one feisty mama bear."

The American cocked his head and narrowed his eyes. "When, exactly, is she going to be a mama bear?"

Looking at his watch, Dante answered, "In about eight months." He tried to be nonchalant, but he couldn't keep the smile from his face.

"No fucking way."

"Yeah. She doesn't want to tell anyone until she's reached the safe point in her pregnancy."

"What the hell is that?"

"Around ten or twelve weeks. She says that's when the chance of miscarriage is reduced drastically."

"You mean you have to keep quiet about this for over another month?" John chuckled. "Yeah, good luck with that, man."

"I can do it. I promised her I would."

"Well, you don't have to worry about me—I can keep a secret."

"I know you can. Speaking of secrets, wanna tell me what's going on with Laila Hernandez?"

"Nope," his friend said, quickly looking away.

"Not even a hint?"

"Not even a hint."

"But I just told you..."

"D, when I have something to tell, I will. There's nothing to share with the class right now."

"Because you're spending all your time here?"

His friend shrugged. "That's probably part of it. There's a lot of factors in play at the moment."

As if to keep Dante from pressing, John changed the subject back to the Mexican's favorite topic—his Bella.

"So how are we going to keep Kennedy safe? Don't you think it's going to draw suspicion that a new woman has moved into your house so quickly?"

"She wants to move back to the States and live a *normal* life." He put his fingers up in air quotes when he said *normal*.

"I think that's a good idea, actually."

"You do?"

John nodded. "Yeah. There's a lot of places you can hide in plain sight, where no one would think twice if you have a little money. You can live comfortably without drawing attention to yourselves. You can't do that here; everyone knows who you are and notices everything you do. In most American cities, as long as you keep a low profile and don't flaunt your money, nobody's going to know who you are or even care enough to try to find out."

He thought about what Kennedy had said earlier, how she wanted her kids to be raised.

"I don't think we could keep a low enough profile to stay off of people's radar. We have to have security, armored cars, house staff..."

"There's a lot of places you can have that and still blend in, as long as you're not obnoxious about it."

He wasn't convinced. Ensenada was a safe haven for him. His family controlled the city, including the police force. Nobody messed with the Guzman cartel in Sinaloa. In American, there would be too much competition with other organized crime families—the Italians, Russians, and Chinese to name a few—not to mention the street gangs. How would he be able to keep his little family safe?

Maybe they could compromise and come back to Mexico once the baby was born. He was confident they could stay hidden in the States, and he could keep Kennedy and the baby safe for the short-term, but for the long-term, they needed to be in Ensenada.

But first, he needed to buy her a new identity. Maybe him too, if he was really going to America.

"What would you think about me running things in San Diego while you took care of business here for a while?"

His friend grinned. "I think that, for you, that can be arranged."

"Maybe you could even bring your cartel princess here for a visit. Impress her."

"Stay out of this, D," John warned.

Dante raised his hands defensively. "I'll mind my own business. I just want you to be as happy as I am, and you seemed like you were when you met her."

The American gave a placating, fake smile but refused to offer anything more.

Dante shrugged. "Suit yourself. Are you staying for this conference call?"

"No, if you don't need me anymore, I'm going to head back to San Diego."

"You want to take the jet?"

"Yeah. Delta or AeroMexico really need to get a direct flight into San Diego. I could drive there faster than the damn airlines can get me there."

"We should look at investing in a long-range helicopter, like Ramon has. Do you think it'd be hard to put a helipad in if I'm just renting a place?"

John shook his head and rolled his eyes.

"Low profile, *vato*. What don't you understand about low profile?"

Chapter Twenty-Eight

Kennedy

As much as she loved the estate in Ensenada, she was excited about getting back to the US. Dante only agreed to go for six months, starting in her third trimester and staying for three months after the baby was born, but she thought it was a fair compromise. It was a start, at least. She wanted to believe he'd love America so much he wouldn't want to leave, but considering he had lived there from the time he was twelve until he turned twenty-six, she wasn't betting on it.

He promised they'd revisit it once the baby was closer to school age.

John was going to stay at the estate and tend to business in Ensenada while they were gone, and Dante was going to concentrate on expanding the dispensaries. Kennedy and Dante still hadn't figured out where they were going to live, although it would most likely be California or Arizona, since they both preferred warmer weather.

She walked into his office, her baby bump still barely visible, and wrapped her arms around his shoulders from behind, kissing his cheek.

"You were up early today."

He spun around in his brown leather chair and pulled her into his lap.

"I took your advice and had a conference call with someone on the East Coast. You're right, we would be a good fit for that market."

That made her smile, then she nervously bit her lip.

"Today is the ten-week mark. I think it's safe to tell people."

He tightened his hold on her hip while a grin lit up his gorgeous face. "Really? My father is going to be so thrilled. If you don't mind, I'd like to invite him for dinner sometime this week so we can tell him together."

"Of course."

She was suddenly filled with sadness at not being able to share the news with her family. For all her mother's flaws, there was never a doubt that she loved Kennedy and Reagan—she would love the opportunity to be a grandmother. And Kennedy missed Reagan. Her sassy, free-spirit sister was the yin to her yang. While their resemblance was striking, the two couldn't have been more different. But they had been close growing up, in spite of the three-year age difference. Reagan would be the perfect eccentric auntie.

"What's wrong, Bella?"

"I miss my family," she said softly with a melancholy smile.

Dante gripped her hand and squeezed.

"The paperwork is almost done, little one. You'll be able to reach out to them soon."

"Babe, this isn't something I can just *reach out* about. I'm going to have to see them in person. They think I'm dead."

"I know, and I've done everything I can on my end. We're just waiting now. But authentic documents take time. My guy has a contact in the passport office—once we get them, they'll be legitimate. Just be patient."

With a sigh and a meek smile, she replied, "I'm trying."

Dante softly kissed her neck.

"Which brings us to the other thing."

She knew what he was referring to, but chose to tease him. "What other thing?"

"Marrying me. You said you would marry me."

"I said that?" She cocked her head. "Are you sure? Had I been drinking?"

"You better not have been drinking in your condition," he growled.

"Then I was probably post-orgasmic. I can't be held responsible for anything I agree to when you've been between my legs. And since I'm not wearing a ring, your story is questionable, at best."

He threw his head back and laughed. She loved the sound of his deep, robust laugh, and the look on his face when he was happy. Seeing him like that filled her with joy.

"Okay, then let me try again. I haven't been between your legs since last night, so you can't use that as an excuse, and..." He paused and kissed her mouth, making a show of smelling her breath. "Nope, no alcohol. That just leaves the ring..."

Dante opened the middle drawer of his desk and pulled out a small, black velvet box, opening it to exhibit a stunning emerald-cut diamond that had to be at least three carats. Tears welled up in her eyes and began to roll down her cheeks when he held her chin firmly in place between his finger and thumb.

"Marry me, Kennedy Alicia Jones."

Of course it wasn't a question. She'd expect nothing less from him.

Keni knew if she answered, it would come out a sob, so she simply nodded her head.

He slid the diamond on her finger, kissing her mouth as he did.

"I love you," she managed to whimper as she wrapped her arms around his neck. "So much."

Dante rested his forehead against hers.

"I love you, too, Bella."

They sat there momentarily, just being in the moment with each other until she could form words without squeaking them out.

"So, are you able to take a break?" she asked, sliding her hands from his neck and running her index finger suggestively over his chest.

With a smirk, he replied, "For my fiancée, I think that can be arranged."

****

Dante

The wedding ceremony would be performed in the middle of estate, almost in the exact position where he'd tackled her when she tried to escape. The irony of the fact that he'd be marrying her on that spot wasn't lost on him.

Fourteen months ago, he never could have predicted he'd have a wife with a baby on the way. Hell, even six months ago, when he'd been relentlessly searching for her with no luck, he wouldn't have guessed it.

The circumstances of how she got pregnant still weighed on him. He often wondered if she would have returned to the estate if she hadn't been pregnant—a concern he voiced on the eve of their wedding as they lounged on his office couch with her sprawled on top of him.

"Dante, I stayed in Mexico even when I didn't know I was pregnant, with the intention of coming back. While the baby was a bit of a surprise, it wasn't a big one, given that was your intention when I was locked in the dungeon, and I knew that was my most fertile time."

"I'm sorry I did that," he whispered.

Her smile was genuine when she entwined her fingers through his.

"I'm not. Not even a little. I'm marrying the love of my life tomorrow and in six months, I'm going to have his baby."

He pulled her closer and growled, "And in two years, you're going to have another one."

With a slap to his shoulder, she chastised, "Whoa, slow down there, hombre. Let's see how this labor goes before you go getting any ideas. You only get one free pass."

"I don't even deserve that—but I'm selfish, so I'll take it."

She situated herself so she was straddling him and started to grind her pussy on his cock, which was now erect under his trousers. She was wearing a skirt, and he lifted it to reveal pink satin and lace panties with a wet spot in the middle.

"Evil temptress," he hissed as he tweaked her nipple. They'd agreed on no sex for the entire two weeks she'd been planning their wedding, and she had purposefully been trying to seduce him every night since they'd made the arrangement. "Why did you suggest it if you didn't want to do it?" he scolded.

"It seemed like a good idea at the time, but now that it's forbidden... I want you even more. Plus, I'm so horny it's not funny."

He tugged on her hips, pushing her pussy further down on his dick under his slacks, and sat up to gently bite her nipples over the fabric of her top.

She started to rock on his cock—he could feel how wet she was, even through the clothing barrier between them.

"Little one, I'm more than happy to break our pact, just say the word."

That caused her to slow her grinding and groan loudly. With a sigh, she rolled off his lap and stood in front of him with her hands on her hips.

"Stop being so sexy," she scolded.

Chuckling as he brought his feet to the floor, he replied, "I'll work on that."

She bent over, one hand on his knee and the other stroking him over his tented pants, and whispered, "I can't wait for you to fuck me so hard tomorrow night."

His smile was placating when he looked up at her. His days of fucking her rough and hard were on hold for a while.

With narrowed eyes, she stood up straight. "What?"

"I told you two weeks ago. I'm not fucking you hard with my baby inside you."

"Oh my god, you are being ridiculous. The doctor said there are no limitations on our sex life. None."

"Don't care. Not risking it."

"Auugh!" She stomped her foot with her hands clenched at her sides, then spun around and marched out.

He couldn't help but chuckle as he called after her, "You're adorable, Kennedy Jones!"

She reappeared in the doorway, glowering at him.

"I'll show you adorable," she said, then disappeared again.

"You just did," he exclaimed, not sure if she was still within earshot.

He couldn't wait to be naked with her again. Her American passport with her new name, Bella Rose Johnson, had arrived and he was taking her to Aruba for their honeymoon the day after they were married.

Now he stood impatiently on the lawn, dressed in his tuxedo, with Father Castellanos standing beside him. John was there too, along with his father, his uncle, Rosa, and Maria—all of them waiting for his Bella to appear at the end of the aisle. When she emerged on the walkway, it literally took his breath away. Her simple ivory-silk strapless dress fit her like a glove, highlighting her round hips and breasts, which were becoming more luscious by the week—and that was saying a lot, since they were pretty succulent to begin with. The gown draped elegantly around her ankles, with a modest train flowing behind her. Her hair, chestnut brown now, was curled and flowing above her shoulders, and his mother's pearl choker highlighted her slender neck. She was absolutely stunning.

And she's all mine.

He could finally breathe when she was standing next to him in front of the priest, and he leaned down to kiss her tenderly on the mouth. Kennedy's hand snaked behind his head, her fingers digging into his hair, while his arm wrapped around her waist, his lips lingering on hers until Father Castallenos coughed.

They pulled apart, laughing, and Dante reached down to hold her hand, only letting go to exchange wedding bands.

This wedding was the one she had asked for, the one where they used her real name. He uttered *Kennedy Alicia Jones* reverently when he said his vows, her eyes watering as he made his promises to her from the heart. He'd never meant anything more than when he pledged to love, honor, and be faithful to her for the rest of his life.

How was this beautiful woman really his wife and carrying his baby?

****

Rosa and Maria had gone all out, making a beautiful six-course meal to celebrate, complete with a two-tier wedding cake decorated in pink frosting flowers. They toasted with champagne—and apple cider for the mama-to-be.

His father was enamored with her, despite her having murdered his brother. Dante suspected her carrying his future grandchild played a big role in that—along with the fact that his brother had been a tyrant. His uncle Ramon was equally smitten by her charms.

John pulled him aside after dinner, offering him a highball glass of Macallan Rare Cask whiskey on the rocks.

Offering his glass up in a toast, the American told him, "You two are perfect for each other. I couldn't be happier for you. May you always be this happy together."

Dante clinked his friend's glass.

"Cheers. And thank you for being the best best friend a man could ask for. I am blessed that you are in my life. I love you like a brother."

"Same here, man. I love you, too."

The two man-hugged, complete with the obligatory two back slaps before pulling apart.

"Should we get back?" John gestured toward the dining room with his glass.

"Probably, before Ramon tries to run off with my bride." Dante stopped and chuckled, shaking his head. "I have a bride."

John slapped him hard on the back then clutched his shoulder, urging him forward. "And don't forget a baby. You're going to be a dad."

"Holy shit," Dante muttered in disbelief.

"You're a lucky son of a bitch, my friend."

The Mexican smiled thoughtfully when they reached the doorway to the room where everyone else was chatting, and watched Kennedy wistfully.

"I certainly am," he murmured before moving to his wife's side.

Chapter Twenty-Nine

Kennedy/Bella

She was in the kitchen laughing with Rosa and Maria, still in her wedding gown, when she glanced up and found him leaning against the doorjamb, his sleeves rolled up—one hand in his pocket, and one hand holding the end of his tuxedo jacket thrown over his shoulder. He was watching her with one corner of his mouth turned up, looking like a model straight out of *GQ* magazine.

"Mrs. Guzman," was all he said. He held his hand out toward her, and she was instantly ready to climb him like a tree. This sexy man was her *husband* and baby daddy.

She said goodnight to the women, and sashayed toward him with a seductive smile.

"Mr. Guzman," she answered, offering him her hand while looking up at him through her lashes.

They made it two steps from the kitchen before he wrapped an arm around her waist and pulled her into him. Looking down at her, he tucked her hair behind her ear.

"Did I tell you how stunning you are in that dress?"

Kennedy shrugged her shoulders coyly as her toes curled.

"Yes, but you can tell me again."

With his lips inches from hers, he whispered, "You are the most beautiful woman I've ever laid eyes on," then enveloped her mouth with his in a kiss so passionate it sent butterflies racing through her insides. She was instantly wet and filled with desire.

"Let's go upstairs, husband," she purred when they came up for air. She had plans for her groom on their wedding night.

"After you, wife."

She gasped when they walked into the bedroom—candles filled the room, along with flowers and rose petals strewn across the floor and bed. In the sitting area, a bucket of sparkling cider sat chilling, two empty flutes on the coffee table between the two wingback chairs.

"Did you do all this?" she asked, whirling around with her arms stretched out in amazement.

"John helped."

"It's so romantic." And not at all what she had originally planned. He'd been handling her with kid gloves since she told him she was pregnant; and frankly, she missed getting fucked into submission. Her intention had been to drive him crazy with desire until he couldn't help but fuck her rough and hard. But this gesture was so sweet and romantic, she was quickly reconsidering her initial idea. Besides, there was always their honeymoon to carry out her plan.

She approached him with slow, deliberate steps, stopping a foot in front of him. Reaching behind her, she slid the zipper down until the dress pooled at her feet, leaving her bare breasts exposed, along with her white thigh stockings and garters. His eyes filled with desire while he drank in her naked body.

Stepping toward her, his hands skimmed her sides and settled on her hips as he whispered in awe, "Bella, you're so beautiful. I can't believe you're my wife."

Ever so gently, he kissed her. It was a sensuous tease that left her wanting more, and she fumbled to unbutton his starched white shirt. The man was perfection—defined abs and just the right amount of chest hair to make him masculine but not hairy. His body, coupled with the scent of his cologne, was sending her hormones into overdrive. With her fingers spread, she ran her hands over his core while kissing his chest.

Dante tilted her chin to capture her lips with his. As he deepened the kiss, she wound her arms around his neck, and he scooped her up to carry her to the bed. After setting her down softly, he removed the rest of his clothes and lay naked next to her, his hand protectively on her stomach.

He began kissing her shoulder, giving her little love bites as he worked down to her breasts. Cupping the right one in his hand, he swirled his tongue around her left nipple and then suckled—kneading her flesh in his other hand before popping her pink tip from his lips and moving to concentrate on her other tit.

Her husband took his time, obviously in no rush despite her lifting her hips in invitation. Finally, gloriously, his fingers starting tracing down her stomach. She reached for his cock to stroke, but Dante moved his hips so his dick was out of her reach.

"Why?" she whined. She wanted to feel his velvety soft rod in her hand.

"Soon, Bella. Let me focus on you right now."

Who was she to argue?

Dante kissed her tummy, pausing to caress her baby bump and lay reverential kisses on it, before moving further down until he reached the apex between her legs. Once there, he licked down the crease of her thigh, ran his tongue from left to right along her pussy, and licked up the crease on the other side. His tease was deliciously torturous, and Kennedy could feel how soaked she was.

She felt him slide further down between her legs, like he was getting comfortable. Using both his hands, he spread her lips apart, then ran one finger up and down her folds.

"You're so wet, Bella."

"I want you, Dante. Please..."

He chuckled softly while he dipped his mouth closer to her sex. "Not yet," he said, then swiped his flat tongue up her slit, making her initially jump, then move her head to the side and moan as she arched her back off the mattress.

"Fuuuuuck..."

"Mmm-hmm," he murmured, and began to work his tongue against her clit. He flicked it furiously at first, making her stomach clench and her body temperature rise, then the bastard slowed his pace and began to leisurely lick her labia up and down.

"You're not supposed to torture your wife on her wedding night," she panted in frustration, lifting her head to watch him smirk while he continued licking her like an ice cream cone.

"I'm not torturing my wife, I'm savoring her," he corrected.

"No, you're torturing me."

He darted his tongue inside her, and she lifted her hips.

Pulling his head back and adjusting his hands to spread her open wider, he stared at her pink center while asking, "Do you want to come, little one?"

"Yes," she whimpered. *Fuck yes!*

"Mmm, okay." He attacked her clit in a frenzy with his tongue while sliding a finger in and out of her hole. Her entire body began to tighten, and her pussy gripped his finger until he could barely move it inside her.

"Come for me, Bella," he demanded as he maintained his oral assault on her hooded knot.

Her orgasm started at her toes and crept up her body until it was racking every cell in her system. She shook and lurched before she started floating back down to Earth.

He tried sucking on her clit, but she furiously pushed his head away while attempting to close her legs.

"Oh my god," she panted, glancing down at him wiping his face on the sheets with a satisfied smile before moving his body on top of hers.

Keni felt his cock line up against her entrance and, with one swift motion, he filled her pussy. They both moaned at the sensation as he pressed further until he was balls deep inside her. Dante began thrusting in and out, his rhythm steady against her still-sensitive clit.

He leaned down and sensually kissed her, their tongues tangling while she framed his handsome face in her hands. Her husband rested on his elbows, relaxed his forehead against hers, and closed his eyes, while he continued moving in and out of her.

"You feel so good, Bella. God, I love you."

His arms encased her body, and he buried his face in her neck as he started to pump harder and faster into her pussy. It felt amazing, and she was soon on the precipice of another orgasm.

"Oh yes, baby," she panted, her nails digging into his back. "Don't stop."

He started to grunt, his breathing labored while he pounded her.

"Yes, yes, yessssss!" she squealed seconds before he thundered a long moan, and she felt rope after rope of his cum hit her walls while his thrusts became uncoordinated.

Clinging to him, she didn't let him move from his position on top of her. She felt too warm and safe and didn't want him to move. He didn't seem to mind, hugging her upper body against his, while his face remained buried in her neck and his cock in her pussy.

Slowly, he began to soften, and he eventually slipped out of her womb, his cum spilling out and running down her thighs. Dante kissed her cheek before rolling off her, disappearing momentarily into the bathroom and returning with a towel, where he carefully tended to cleaning her up.

"You're so fucking sexy, Mrs. Guzman."

She sat up, drawing the covers to her chest.

"It's my husband. He turns me on."

That elicited a laugh as he slid in next to her and pulled her close.

"Get some rest. We've got to get up early for our flight."

Seven glorious days in a bungalow on the beach with her husband's undivided attention... she couldn't wait.

****

Dante

They were wheels up for Aruba by eleven a.m. the next morning, he and Bella Johnson. He really needed to get in the habit of referring to her by her new last name. They'd decided the wedding ceremony was just for them, and the paperwork that was now safely in his vault reflected their real names. They'd have another one that they'd actually record with the government after enough time had passed that it wouldn't rouse suspicion he had married someone other than Kennedy Jones.

But it really would be a lot easier when she was Bella Guzman, and he'd probably just call her that anyway. Especially this week, since they weren't hiding that they were on their honeymoon. He was looking forward to seeing her relax and not be endlessly looking over her shoulder.

He asked John to make contact with the associates who'd brokered the exchange of Kennedy's real name over a year ago. Dante wanted to know if the CIA had her listed as deceased or not. If they did, it would go a long way in alleviating her constant worry—and hopefully allow her to get out more. She was slowly becoming a pregnant hermit, and the light in her eyes was going out.

"I'm sure when the baby comes, things will change," John offered.

"Not if she's afraid to let her guard down. With the baby, it'll probably make it worse."

"Maybe being in a new city will be good for her. Have you considered moving sooner than her third trimester? That's kind of an uncomfortable time for a woman to be unpacking boxes, D."

"My wife isn't going to be unpacking a damn thing. We're buying all brand-new furniture and home furnishings, along with any clothes or personal items she needs."

"She's still going to have to organize all that, dumbass."

"Well, then I'll hire a personal assistant for her."

"You still should consider going sooner."

Dante grinned. "Are you in that big of a hurry to move into my place?"

"Actually, no. The fact that I'm moving to Ensenada is really fucking up my personal life."

"Are you still dating Laila?"

His friend frowned. "Nah. She's a little higher maintenance than I have time for."

"How was the sex?"

"It was... decent."

"Decent?"

John shrugged.

The Mexican chuckled. "Well, I'm glad you're no longer dating her then. Life's too short to settle for *decent* sex. Even if it is Miguel Hernandez's daughter. I hope that doesn't come back to bite us in the ass though."

"Don't worry about it. She broke it off with me. It was amicable."

Dante got the feeling there was a lot more to this story and wanted to press for details, but at the look on the American's face, he decided to drop it.

They had yet to receive confirmation from their contact in the CIA, despite having paid another hefty sum upfront. The son of a bitch had taken more money from the cartel than the man—or his children's children—could spend in their lifetimes. Still, Dante felt confident he and Bella were safe in Aruba, and he was going to see to it that they enjoyed themselves thoroughly.

In and out of bed.

Chapter Thirty

Bella

They'd checked into their bungalow on the beach—just her and Dante. She'd wavered back and forth between being glad they hadn't brought security staff with them, so they wouldn't draw attention, and feeling vulnerable that the men weren't there to watch over them.

The feeling vulnerable part was the most distressing—she was still a badass, dammit, with or without the government credentials. She didn't need Dante's men to keep her safe, but she now had a tiny person growing inside her to think about. The fact that her own agency had tried to kill her had unsettled her in a way she'd never experienced.

She walked through their hut, checking the locks on the windows and looking for other ways someone could penetrate their temporary space. Dante grabbed her wrist the third time she walked by him sitting on the couch, and pulled her into his lap.

"Little one, you need to relax. No one knows we're here. No one."

She knew he was right. They'd taken precautions: using one of his associate's planes instead of his; their reservations made under her new name, not his. They'd been paying for everything in cash or with her fancy new MasterCard with the name Bella R. Johnson on the front, and the billing address was one of his dummy corporations which—last she recollected from his file she had known by heart—the agency had no knowledge of.

"I know. I really wish I could have a drink. That would help me calm down."

He started rubbing her shoulders and the back of her neck.

"Go get undressed and lie on the bed, let me give you a massage."

He'd never made such an offer before, but in her experience, when a man volunteered to rub her back, it was implied he wanted to rub a lot more than just that. So when he actually just massaged her back, neck, and shoulders without attempting to touch her anywhere else, she was somewhat offended.

Then her pregnant hormonal feelings became hurt, and she began to cry.

It took him a moment to realize she had tears streaming down her face, but once he did, he scooped her up into his arms and began to gently rock her against him.

"Bella, what on earth is wrong?"

"You don't want me anymore," she wailed.

"What in god's name are you talking about, woman?" He placed her hand over his hard-on. "Does that feel like I don't want you? I always want you—it worries me how much, sometimes."

She sniffled against his chest, asking softly, "You do? Still? Even though I'm pregnant?"

"Oh, Bella. *Especially* because you're pregnant."

"Then why won't you fuck me?"

"I've told you, I'm not risking it. But once the baby comes, I'm taking you away and tying you to the bed and abusing you for a week straight, and I'll use zip ties so you can't escape."

She smirked as she wiped her eyes with her fingertips. "I can get out of those too, you know. Just not as easily."

"You might have to prove it."

Biting her bottom lip, she looked up at him through her wet lashes. "But what if I don't want to?"

He growled as he began to fondle her tits and tweak her nipples. "You dirty girl."

"You should probably punish me…"

****

Dante

She was making it so difficult to be gentle with her, and he almost caved and put her over his knee. Then he thought how devastated he would feel if something happened to their little one. Even if it wasn't because of rough play, he knew he'd still feel responsible. He was going to handle her with care until Junior was safe and sound in the nursery crib, and she was healed.

Then he was going to fuck her into submission like the good old days.

Bella fought back a yawn, and Dante lay back on the pillows, gesturing for her to nestle in next to him.

"I just need a little nap," she murmured. "Please don't leave me alone. I sleep much better knowing you're lying next to me."

Hearing that did wonders for his ego. His little badass needed him in order to feel safe.

Then she added, "And you should probably be naked, too," and he was no longer as convinced. But he did as she requested and stripped down to his boxer briefs.

"Underwear doesn't equal naked," she chastised as she put her arm around his center.

"Underwear means you'll take a nap," he corrected.

She sighed dramatically. "Spoilsport."

He laughed out loud and lightly tapped her on the ass. "Go to sleep."

And she did. He noticed that she was tired a lot lately—which only made sense; she *was* literally forming another human in her body.

He dozed off next to her, and when he woke his hands were above his head. It was when he tried to scratch his balls that he realized he couldn't move them from their position over his head.

"What the fuck?" he snarled, scanning the room. A sense of dread that something had happened to his wife overwhelmed him.

She came out of the bathroom and smiled when she noticed he was awake.

"Hey, sleepyhead."

"Kennedy Alicia Guzman, what the fuck do you think you're doing?"

"Oh, just a little payback," she smirked as she crawled up on the bed and sat next to where he was held captive.

His eyebrows furrowed. "What do you mean, *payback*?"

"For my time in the dungeon—which, now that I'm your wife, you need to show me how to access, as well as the room below it."

"How do you know about the panic room on the first floor?"

She huffed out an exasperated breath and rolled her eyes.

"It doesn't take having an MBA from Stanford to figure that out, babe. I know all the secrets of the estate, except how to get in and out of your dungeon. That knowledge would have been particularly useful about three months ago, by the way, so I'm hoping you'll unlock that mystery for me should I need it in the future."

He'd thought about that—beaten himself up over it, actually. It weighed heavily on him, especially when she had still been missing.

"I should have shown you how to access the rooms before I left for San Diego. I'm so sorry. You would have been safe. The downstairs room has an escape tunnel leading to the garage."

"That would have definitely helped."

He wanted to caress her face, and he tugged on his restraints.

"I'm sorry I wasn't there to protect you. We'll get your facial recognition into the software first thing when we get back, and I'll show you how to get into the rooms, as well as the staircase and tunnel."

Her expression turned sad, although she attempted a smile.

"Sometimes I let myself forget how you make your living, but then things like this remind me how dangerous it's going to be for our child."

Dante lifted his upper body off the bed as much as he could to emphasize what he was about to say.

"I swear to you, I will do everything in my power to make sure you and the baby are always safe and protected."

She looked into his eyes for a moment without saying anything. Then, with a genuine, small smile, she kissed his cheek and whispered, "I know you will."

Scooting further down his body, she began to tug on his boxer briefs.

"Now, about this payback..."

****

Bella

His cock was only semi-erect as she tugged his underwear down his thighs. She knew he was going to have a hard time letting her be in charge, and an even harder time giving up complete control—hence the handcuffs. Now he had no choice.

"Whatever shall I do with you?" she purred, slithering down his body. She kissed his core, and as her pebbled nipples softly grazed his hip, she felt him harden under her. "Well, hello there."

Licking down his shaft, she kept going until she was nestled between his legs and began to mouth his balls—tugging on the skin with her lips while he groaned his approval.

"Damn, Bella, that feels so fucking good."

She let her tongue explore further, pushing his legs apart so she could properly lick his taint. As her tongue darted between his balls and his ass, she proceeded to slowly stroke his cock, smearing the precum around his tip with her thumb. Feeling drunk with power, she gathered his balls in one hand and fit them both in her mouth at once, running her tongue back and forth over the skin.

"Holy fuck, that's hot," he growled, and she glanced up to find him watching her every move intently. A small smile managed to escape her full mouth, and she slowly released his sac with a *pop*.

"Mmm, I love how you smell," she cooed, licking the underside of his balls while they rested on her nose.

"You are a dirty, dirty girl, Mrs. Guzman."

Rubbing her pussy against his leg, she murmured between licks, "I think we've already established that, Mr. Guzman."

"My cock is so hard for you."

Bella began to tug his shaft harder. "Oh, I can feel that," she said, then sat up so she was straddling his hips, his cock in her hands between her legs. With a smirk, she reached over to the nightstand and pulled out a jar of coconut oil, letting the contents drizzle all over him until his dick was glistening.

"So slippery," she commented as she began to leisurely jerk him with both hands, moving her eyes between his gorgeous face and his steel prick while rocking her hips in a slow tempo on top of his.

She'd chosen coconut oil so she could still suck him, as the taste was quite pleasant. Drizzling more of the natural lubricant on him before slipping between his legs again, she rubbed the runaway oil up along his taint and further toward his ass.

To her surprise, he didn't jump when she ventured her finger into his crack.

Bobbing her head up and down on his shaft, Bella took him deep in her throat and held him there as she breached his back door with her finger. She was enjoying having him at her mercy. He didn't freeze or clench beneath her, so she began to work her finger in unison with her mouth and hand on his shaft, which was hard as granite.

Dante's breathing was starting to become irregular, and his throaty groans were turning into grunts, so she began to moan around his cock in her throat. He always loved that.

"Fuuuuck, I'm going to come soon if you don't stop."

That only made her double down with her efforts: moaning louder; slurping, sucking, stroking, and probing faster and firmer; subtly rubbing her soaked pussy against his hairy thigh in the process. It was such a turn-on for her to blow him, and being in charge like this was only adding to it. The fact that he hadn't fought her for control made her feel honored—she knew that had to have taken a lot of trust on his part.

With a loud groan, he began to thrust up, and she tasted his salty cum.

"That's it, take it all," he demanded as rope after rope spurted down her throat.

She pulled him out of her mouth and wiggled her finger in his ass before removing it, admonishing him with a smirk, "So bossy."

"Uncuff me so I can show you who's really in charge."

"Tsk, tsk. I don't think so."

Bella moved up to straddle his chest, putting another pillow under his head so he had a good view of her pussy, spread wide and just out of reach of his mouth. Dante began to tug on his restraints with more fervor.

"You better take these goddamn handcuffs off me now, woman," he warned in a low growl.

Grinding against his chest, she began to rub her clit in circles, defiantly asking, "Or what?"

"I'm gonna paint your ass red."

That only made her massage her knot faster. "Oh, baby, you say the sweetest things."

He quit tugging and began to watch her pleasure herself, mesmerized at the sight.

"You dirty slut, you know you want to sit on my face and grind your cunt on my mouth. Come on, baby, let me fuck you with my tongue."

The thought made her moan out loud, and her juices began to smear all over his chest as she rolled her hips on him.

Dante lifted his neck, moaning, "Mmm, fuck, baby. I can smell how good you'd taste. Please? Sit on my face."

She reached behind herself to fondle his cock, and found him already hard again.

"So many options," she cooed as she stroked his length up and down, exposing herself even wider.

"Look how fucking wet you are. God, I need to taste you. Come on, little one, ride your husband's face."

Releasing his cock, she scooted forward so her entrance lined up with his mouth. At first, she planned on teasing him, but he lurched his neck forward and began to tonguefuck her with a vengeance. Any thought of teasing him flew right out the window. His mouth felt so good on her pussy, it was like she was in a trance.

"Uncuff me, Bella, so I can play with your clit."

All she was thinking about was him rubbing her jewel, so it wasn't until she heard the click of the hinge that she realized what she'd just done.

To her surprise, and perhaps slight disappointment, he didn't move to punish her. Instead he did exactly as promised, and devoured her pussy while polishing her clit, quickly bringing her to a delicious climax.

Only after she'd finished shuddering did Dante pounce, flipping her onto her hands and knees while wrapping a hand around her neck and snarling into her ear, "You naughty, naughty bitch. I'm going to teach you a lesson." He immediately thrust inside her—hard, gripping her hips as he filled her over and over, slamming balls deep without mercy. Exactly what she'd been needing. He smacked her ass as he relentlessly pounded her pussy.

Best punishment ever.

Then she felt the slippery coconut oil drip into her ass crack, and the excitement and anticipation for what she knew was coming sent her into another orgasm that was even more intense than the first one.

She hadn't finished catching her breath when he slid out of her pussy and slowly breached her star. It was an odd sensation—more so than the butt plug he had used on her—and her whole body tingled, then broke out into goosebumps as he began to pump her ass.

"Your ass is as tight as your cunt. Fuuuuck, I can't decide which I like more."

Her husband reached under her and slid two fingers inside, filling her completely full.

"I'm going to fuck you with your dildo next time I fuck your ass."

"Oh my god, yesssss!"

She felt him chuckle in her ear. "You dirty whore. I knew you'd like that idea."

He began to fingerfuck her faster as he thrust deeper into her butt, making her cry out while she quivered around his fingers with her third orgasm of the night. He sat up on his knees and, with his fingers digging into her hips, held her tight while driving into her until he began to grunt with his own orgasm.

"Holy fuck," he panted as he collapsed on top of her.

Within seconds, he gathered her in his arms, kissing her hair, forehead, and cheeks with a worried look.

"Did I hurt you, Bella? I'm so sorry. You just had me crazy with desire, I—"

She put two fingers to his lips, silencing him.

"You didn't hurt me. It was amazing, and I loved every second. I came three times, for goodness sake. The baby is fine, I'm fine, and as a matter of fact, I'm going to insist you do that again before we leave."

The corner of his mouth lifted, and he slowly shook his head. "My perfect wife."

"Does that mean I get to be in charge again?" she asked hopefully.

"We'll see."

She knew what *we'll see* meant. That was okay. She still had the handcuffs.

Epilogue One—*Slow Burn*

Bella

They'd decided to move to San Diego, so she was in California trying to get everything prepared. She and Dante had been looking online and had narrowed their choices down to three homes. Two were in Rancho Santa Fe, and the third was in prestigious La Jolla Farms, where John lived.

She was staying with John while Dante tended to business in Ensenada, and the community was fast becoming her favorite. Her daughter's future godfather was helping her look at the houses, as well as hire a personal assistant. They'd conducted three interviews and were waiting for the last candidate to arrive at John's small, nondescript office downtown.

"I liked the second one the best so far, I think," she told him as she rested her swollen ankles on the turquoise blue ottoman and leaned her head on the back of the orange leather sofa in the sitting area of John's bright, modern office. It was a vast difference from Dante's traditional rich mahogany and burgundy leather workspace.

He made a face. "She seemed a little needy. Like she's going to have a breakdown when she's let go in six months, even though you've been upfront with her about it being a temporary assignment."

Bella chewed the side of her mouth. "Maybe. But she seemed to be the most open to taking direction."

John appeared to be contemplating what she'd said when his secretary announced the arrival of the last candidate over intercom.

"Send her in," he called from his seat behind his sleek, U-shaped, glass-topped steel desk.

Mrs. Guzman was lost in thought—pondering his assessment of the second candidate as needy and admiring his orange executive chair—so she happened to be watching his face when the next candidate walked in. She was fairly certain John had just fallen in love at first sight, although he masked it quickly, rising out his seat and offering his hand in a professional handshake.

"Hi. Please come in. John Turner."

"Quinn Carter," came the demure voice.

The dark-haired woman was older than the rest of the candidates had been—maybe late thirties, possibly early forties—and she was fucking stunning. Normally that would have been an instant hard *no* from Bella, especially considering that she was feeling as big as a house after her belly had popped out, seemingly overnight. It had happened last week, prompting Dante to start the ball rolling for their move. Now, watching the obvious chemistry between the two in front of her, there was no way she could rule Quinn Carter out simply because she was too beautiful. Besides, Bella knew Dante only had eyes for her; she was just feeling insecure because nothing fit her anymore.

John gestured to where she still sat with her feet up, having not moved from her resting position on the couch.

"And that lovely woman is who you'll be working for. She's going to be delivering my niece in three months and is going to be needing assistance with their move."

Bella started to move her feet off the ottoman when Quinn quickly put her hands up.

"Oh, please don't get up on my account."

John was at the raven-haired beauty's side and gestured toward the sitting area. "Won't you please sit down?" He didn't take his eyes off the candidate the entire interview. She'd never seen her friend so smitten before.

Well, I guess I have a new assistant. I hope she passes her background check, for John's sake.

Epilogue Two—*Combustion*

Bella/Kennedy

"Kennedy, is that really you?" her mother whispered, grasping Bella's cheeks between her hands.

"Hi, Mama," she said softly.

"Keni? How is this possible?" Reagan sobbed, hugging a very pregnant Bella in the doorway under the metal green awning that doubled as a carport.

"It's a long story. Would you mind if we came in?" Dante answered for her as they stood on the worn grey industrial carpeting on the steps leading into her mother's trailer.

Her sister—the naïve, sweeter, younger version of Kennedy—was there that Saturday morning to take her mother grocery shopping. Kennedy—Bella—had known she would be. Her mother had named them after her favorite presidents, although neither girl could understand how Delilah Jones could make that determination, since John Kennedy had died the year the woman was born, and she was a twenty-something during the Ronald Reagan era. Her younger sibling still lived in Fargo—although in a better part of town now—and taught art courses at the community center, and graphic design at Minnesota State Community and Technical College's campus nearby.

The Guzmans arrived in a rented white Toyota Camry sedan, trying to be as nondescript as possible so as not to draw the attention of the nosy neighbors in the trailer park. She wore dark sunglasses, but made sure her brown hair was uncovered. Dante had dressed in dark jeans, black Under Armour running shoes, a grey Minnesota Vikings sweatshirt, and a matching baseball cap. She had giggled when he'd finished getting dressed in the hotel that morning. She'd never seen him in sports gear of any type—it was totally not his style. Now that she thought about it, she didn't think she'd ever even seen him in a sweatshirt, and he'd only worn jeans a handful of times while with her—although to his credit, he could rock a pair of Levi's like nobody's business.

Bella waddled inside, past the dining room/kitchen combo with the cracked linoleum, and dropped onto the floral-patterned upholstered couch with a thud. Her mother stayed glued to one side of her while her sister sat on the other. Dante sat down in the hunter green fake-leather recliner, taking in her childhood home. It hadn't changed much in the sixteen years since she'd been gone.

It was a far cry from the mansion Ruby Rhodes had claimed to have grown up in, but Dante had seen pictures—taken by the private investigator he'd hired once he found out her true name—so he already knew about this part of her life. Still, she could tell he wasn't prepared to see first-hand just how poor she'd really been, although he was doing his best to disguise his shock.

Explaining her situation to her mother and sister proved easier than she'd thought, once their astonishment at finding her alive wore off and acceptance sank in. Bella wasn't worried about her sister spilling her secret, and after Dante spelled out for them what it would mean for her to be discovered alive, she felt certain her mother would go to the grave with her secret—especially now that she had a granddaughter on the way.

Reagan rubbed her beach-ball belly affectionately. "I can't believe I'm going to be an auntie!" Then she stopped abruptly. "I will still get to be an auntie, won't I? How is this going to work, Keni?"

"Well, for starters, you're going to have to start calling me by my new name, Bella." In jest, and partly because she had no idea how it was going to work, she added, "Maybe I can be the long-lost daughter Mama gave up for adoption."

Dante sat up straight and shook his head. "No. There can be no official familial relationship to you. Being married to me, it would not take any time for someone to figure out who you really are."

She knew he was absolutely right. They'd talked about it at length before coming here, yet still she found herself whispering, "There has to be a way, Dante."

"There will be, little one. Just not in the traditional sense. When you get together, it will be when we meet on vacations. We already took a big chance coming here, we can't risk that again."

Her mother looked confused, and panic rose up in her voice. "What does that mean?"

Reagan chimed in. "It means, Mama, that when we spend time with Ken—er, Bella and her family, it will be at a neutral location that none of us are tied to. Like we could meet on a cruise for birthdays or at a lodge for the holidays, that kind of thing."

"So I won't be able to just go and watch my granddaughter at her piano recital?"

What the fuck did she just say? The woman had never once gone to any of the extra-curricular activities either of her daughters had participated in.

Delilah grabbed Bella's hand and, with tears in her eyes, said softly, "I know what you're thinking, but I was really hoping to get a second chance with my grandchildren."

Bella's teary eyes matched her mother's, and she lightly squeezed the older woman's hand.

"I'm sorry, Mama. Maybe we can figure something out when the time comes. But it's not like we're just going to be up the street anyway."

Her mom offered a conciliatory smile.

"So I'm having a granddaughter. When are you due?"

"In ten weeks."

"Have you picked out a name yet?"

"Madison Belle Guzman."

Delilah clapped her hands. "Oh, you're naming her after a Founding Father and our fourth president. Thank you for doing that."

"I liked the idea of her having that connection to our family."

"Me too," Reagan chimed in.

Bella stifled a yawn, and Dante stood.

"I think my wife needs to rest, but perhaps we can have dinner at our hotel. It'd have to be in the room, but you'd be able to spend more time together."

"Could you come to my house?" her sister asked. "I have a garage so you could park your car inside, and my neighbors tend to keep to themselves." Her sister wrinkled her nose. "I know it's another trip for you, but just the idea of sitting around on a hotel bed while we try to avoid tripping over each other makes me claustrophobic."

Dante opened his mouth, but Bella cut him off. She knew he was going to interject that they were in the penthouse suite, which had more than enough room—hell, it was bigger than her mother's entire trailer. But her family didn't need to know how wealthy she now was. Not yet, anyway.

Besides, her mother had hit a payday after Kennedy's alleged death.

"Mama, what did you do with the life insurance money and my pension?"

Delilah shot Reagan a death glare. *Oh, that's right.* Kennedy had set up a trust and appointed her sister as executor. That way her mother wouldn't let her next boyfriend take all the money and disappear.

"She's going to get a new trailer and furniture next year with the interest the trust earns."

Bella looked at her mom with a smile. "That'll be nice. Just another reason you need to make sure no one finds out I'm alive—otherwise you'll have to pay all that money back."

Maybe that would help motivate her family to keep quiet, in case her safety wasn't enough.

****

Dante

He wanted to drive Bella straight to Saks Fifth Avenue and buy her every damn item of clothing in her size, every handbag, bottle of perfume, and anything else her heart desired. Seeing in person how she had grown up made him want to grab her, hug her, and whisper she would never worry or want for anything ever again. He'd always take care of her and their daughter, but she already knew that—at least, she'd better.

"Not quite the mansion I told you about when we first met, huh?" she said with a small smile as she leaned back against the headrest.

"I already knew how you grew up, baby, remember?"

"I know, but it's different in pictures."

He shrugged. "So what? It's part of what made you who you are."

"That's true. It was definitely inspiration to study and work my ass off."

Dante smirked, turning into the hotel parking lot.

"Well, not *off*, thank God, because I happen to love your ass."

She backhanded his chest with her left hand just as he put the Camry in park.

"You're hilarious."

He captured her hand in his, bringing it to his lips and kissing her fingertips.

"Seriously, Bella, you're incredible. What you've accomplished, how hard you've worked... you're going to be an amazing mother. Our daughter is one lucky little girl."

The pregnant woman wiggled her pinky finger at him.

"She's going to have you wrapped around her little finger, you know."

"Just like her mama."

Her eyes filled with tears, something that happened a lot since she had become pregnant.

"I love you. Thank you for taking such good care of me."

The Mexican leaned over and softly kissed her lips.

"You deserve it, little one."

****

Bella

Madison Belle Guzman arrived at eight pounds exactly—three days past her due date, by Caesarean section. They stayed at their home in San Diego for a month until Bella felt well enough to travel to Ensenada for a visit to the estate and for the baby's baptism.

Dante brought her sister and mother to Mexico via a cruise ship, booking them a week at Villas Emilio, a rental villa, so Reagan could be Madison's godmother, alongside John as godfather. Quinn traveled with the Guzmans, and although neither she nor John would admit there was anything going on between them, Bella and Dante both knew something was happening. Things definitely got interesting when El Rey and his daughter Laila arrived early for the baptism and stayed in Ensenada, at the villa neighboring Villas Emilio. Dante insisted they stay out of it, but the new mother was secretly rooting for Quinn.

Reagan was supposed to meet them at the mansion for the baptism rehearsal with Father Castellanos and John, but she was very late. They were waiting for her on the patio when Bella's phone started to ring, indicating she had a video call.

"Oh, it's my sister," she said, handing Madison to Dante and walking away with the still-ringing phone to a quieter area.

"Hey, baby sister, everything okay?"

The younger version of herself appeared on her screen, tears streaming down her face. Bella couldn't identify where Reagan was calling from—it didn't look like anywhere at the villa.

"No." Then the redhead started to sob. "I'm so sorry."

Bella's stomach dropped, but she tried to remain calm.

"Honey, it's okay. Just tell me what's wrong."

Her sister just kept sobbing, "I'm sorry," until the camera moved, and she was now looking at a new face. A handsome male face—one she was familiar with.

Mr. East Coast, from the night of her abduction.

"Hello, Agent Jones. Glad to see you're alive and well."

Combustion
Ensenada Heat, Book 2

She was meant to be mine—I knew it the moment I met her. Too bad I'm about to kidnap her.

Mason Hughes

As a decorated CIA agent, I know better than to kidnap a former colleague's sister and hold her hostage on a ship in the middle of the ocean. The agency tends to frown on that sort of behavior. But desperate times call for desperate measures; I have my reasons, and they're good ones. I'll be forgiven with a slap to the wrist—at least for that part of the mission.

Until I tie Reagan Jones up and can't resist her when she presses her tight little body against mine. That's probably not so forgivable.

Then there's the issue of falling in love with her and refusing to let her go once the mission is over. Definitely not forgivable.

I have no idea what I'm thinking—we can't be together; it's not safe for her. I'm a spy, and she's a feisty art instructor from Fargo. Not exactly the perfect match.

Or is it?

Get your copy of *Combustion*
https://www.amazon.com/dp/B07PLMK5DM

Other Works by Tess Summers

Free Book! *The Playboy and the SWAT Princess*

BookHip.com/SNGBXD Sign up here to receive my newsletter, and get SWAT Captain Craig Baxter's love story, exclusively for newsletter subscribers. You'll receive regular updates (but I won't bombard you with emails, I promise), and be the first to know about my works-in-progress. (Like when Ben's story is coming out!)

She's a badass SWAT rookie, and he's a playboy SWAT captain… who's taming who?

Maddie Monroe

Three things you should not do when you're a rookie, and the only female on the SDPD SWAT Team… 1) Take your hazing personally, 2) Let them see you sweat, and 3) Fall for your captain.

Especially, when your captain is the biggest playboy on the entire police force.

I've managed to follow rules one and two with no problem… but the third one I'm having a little more trouble with. Every time he smiles that sinful smile or folds his muscular arms when explaining a new technique or walks through the station full of swagger….

All I can think about is how I'd like to give him my V-card, giftwrapped with a big red bow on it, which is such a bad idea because out of Rules One, Two, and Three, breaking the third one is a sure-fire way to get me kicked off the team and writing parking tickets for the rest of my career.

Apparently my heart—and other body parts—didn't get the memo.

Craig Baxter

The first time I noticed Maddie Monroe, she was wet and covered in soapy suds as she washed SWAT's armored truck as part of her hazing ritual. I've been hard for her ever since.

I can't sleep with a subordinate—it would be career suicide, and I've worked too damn hard to get where I am today. Come to think of it, so has she, and she'd probably have a lot more to lose.

So, nope, not messing around with Maddie Monroe. There are plenty of women for me to choose from who don't work for me.

Apparently my heart—and other body parts—didn't get the memo.

Can two hearts—and other body parts—overcome missed memos and find a way to be together without career-ending consequences?

Operation Sex Kitten

Ava Ericson thought she had her life planned out: graduate with her Ph.D., marry Brad Miller when he finished law school, have 2.5 babies... and mediocre sex for the rest of her days. But when Brad dumps her upon learning he's passed the bar, citing new "opportunities" available, she has to rethink her future.

Believing her lack of experience was the reason Brad broke up with her, she launches Operation Sex Kitten (OSK), a plan to become a vixen in bed and get Brad back. Things might go astray when she meets the notorious attorney, Travis Sterling, the bachelor who she is sure can teach her a thing or two in the bedroom. As she enjoys putting OSK theories into practice, she realizes the real 'operation' will be for the two not to fall in love.

Fun and romantic, *Operation Sex Kitten* turns up the heat with explicit scenes while you root for love to conquer all.

The General's Desire

Ron

I'm a decorated Marine general who doesn't have time for relationships. I've tried—they just don't work out—and I've never lost sleep over it. Then I meet her. Brenna is easily the most beautiful woman I've ever laid eyes on. The first time she blushes under my stare, it's game over. She's going to need to learn that I'm in charge and trust that I always mean what I say because I'm not letting her go.

Brenna

When Ron offers me a drink at the Sterling's wedding reception, I have no idea that he's a military star on the rise, I just know he's the walking definition of masculine—that translates in the bedroom (and couches, counters, tables...) as the best sex I've ever had. The more time we spend together, the more I'm convinced he's hiding something—or someone—and I'm not going down that road again. He can say anything he wants, but actions speak louder than words.

Playing Dirty

Cassie

I'm a career woman. I wear success like a second skin, and I'm rarely satisfied with anything less than the best. This includes my love life. If you want to date me, you better bring your A game because I don't play with the B team.

The only type of commitment I'm interested in is the one I have with my career. There is no man strong enough to tame me. Bold enough to rattle me. Or confident enough to win my heart. But then again, I have never met a man like Luke Rivas.

Luke

Cassie is one feisty, fiery, demanding woman who has enough confidence to intimidate even the bravest of men. She's driven, ambitious, and clearly has no interest in anything more than a casual fling.

But here's the thing. I want her, and once I have her, there will be nothing casual about it.

I will crack through that tough exterior she wears so well and bend her into submission. I'll make her break every one of her own damn rules just for me. And in order to accomplish just that...

I'm willing to play dirty.

Cinderella and the Marine

One night. No strings attached. What could go wrong?

Cooper

I was pretty happy living the carefree life of a successful bachelor. Money to spend, a revolving door of women, no commitment, no relationship troubles—it was perfect. At least, that's what I thought until I held my friends' newborn baby in my arms, and she smiled at me.

That was the moment I realized what life was all about. That was also the moment it occurred to me I needed a baby mama—stat.

So... the hunt is on for the perfect candidate. But first, I might have to have one last fling—you know, go out with a bang. Literally.

Kate

Thanks to making a few wrong decisions along the way, I'm now busting my ass waiting tables while putting myself through college. It's not ideal, but I'm determined to stand on my own two feet and take care of my responsibilities the best I can.

But I'm still a woman. I have needs. I just don't have the time for any kind of commitment. Naturally, when a smoldering hot Marine offers me a no-strings-attached one-night stand, I'm all on board.

Turns out... he wants more than I'm willing to give.

About the Author

Tess Summers is a former businesswoman and teacher who always loved writing but never seemed to have time to sit down and write a short story, let alone a novel. Now battling MS, her life changed dramatically, and she has finally slowed down enough to start writing all the stories she's been wanting to tell, including the fun and sexy ones!

Married over twenty years with three grown children, Tess is a former dog foster mom who ended up failing and adopting them instead. She and her husband (and their six dogs) split their time between the desert of Arizona and the lakes of Michigan, so she's always in a climate that's not too hot and not too cold, but just right!

Contact Me!

Sign up for my newsletter: BookHip.com/SNGBXD
Email: TessSummersAuthor@yahoo.com
Visit my website: www.TessSummersAuthor.com
Follow me (but I tend to be a little naughty on social media!)
Facebook: http://facebook.com/TessSummersAuthor
Twitter: http://twitter.com/@mmmTess
Instagram: https://www.instagram.com/tesssummers/
Amazon: https://amzn.to/2MHHhdK
BookBub https://www.bookbub.com/profile/tess-summers
Book+Main: https://bookandmainbites.com/TessSummers
Goodreads - https://www.goodreads.com/TessSummers